Writing a modern-day version of "The Princess and the Pea" came quite naturally to me. You see, I have great empathy for anyone who can't sleep at night because I have the very same problem. For years my good friends Iris Johansen and Kay Hooper have called me "the princess and the pea."

When I travel with Iris and Kay, I get a room all to myself, one with a king-size bed. I order five extra pillows (don't ask) and always carry a sleep machine (not that it helps). If I can't sleep, I'll wander into Iris and Kay's room, and Kay will talk to me until I get drowsy. Every once in a while Iris will wake up, ask us what we're talking about, mutter something really incoherent, and then instantly fall back to sleep. Iris can fall asleep anytime, anywhere—an ability that irritates me no end.

When I'm home, Iris and Kay are a big help, too, even though we live in different states. If it's one o'clock in the morning and the David Letterman show is over, I can call either of them. Iris isn't a lot of fun, though, because she's asleep and doesn't really know what she's saying. Kay, on the other hand, is great. There's something about her voice that after a while will lull me to sleep—which insults her enormously, but for which I'm very grateful.

At any rate, you can see why I have immense sympathy both for my heroine who suffers from insomnia and for that long-ago princess with her troublesome pea.

Fayrene Preston

WHAT ARE *LOVESWEPT* ROMANCES?

They are stories of true romance and touching emotion. We believe those two very important ingredients are constants in our highly sensual and very believable stories in the *LOVESWEPT* line. Our goal is to give you, the reader, stories of consistently high quality that may sometimes make you laugh, sometimes make you cry, but are always fresh and creative and contain many delightful surprises within their pages.

Most romance fans read an enormous number of books. Those they truly love, they keep. Others may be traded with friends and soon forgotten. We hope that each *LOVESWEPT* romance will be a treasure—a "keeper." We will always try to publish

LOVE STORIES YOU'LL NEVER FORGET
BY AUTHORS YOU'LL ALWAYS REMEMBER

The Editors

589

Fayrene Preston

The Princess and the Pea

BANTAM BOOKS

NEW YORK · TORONTO · LONDON · SYDNEY · AUCKLAND

THE PRINCESS AND THE PEA

A Bantam Book / January 1993

If you would be interested in receiving protective vinyl covers for your Loveswept books, please write to this address for information:

Loveswept
Bantam Books
P.O. Box 985
Hicksville, NY 11802

ISBN 0-553-44171-X

Published simultaneously in the United States and Canada

Bantam Books are published by Bantam Books, a division of Bantam Doubleday Dell Publishing Group, Inc. Its trademark, consisting of the words "Bantam Books" and the portrayal of a rooster, is Registered in U.S. Patent and Trademark Office and in other countries. Marca Registrada. Bantam Books, 666 Fifth Avenue, New York, New York 10103.

PRINTED IN THE UNITED STATES OF AMERICA

OPM   0 9 8 7 6 5 4 3 2 1

The Princess and the Pea

One

In the ethereal twilight of the Alabama evening, Melisande Lanier stood beside her dusty, battered station wagon, drew a deep breath, and smiled. The air smelled the same as she remembered, a perfumed drift of roses, jasmine, and wisteria. The scent conjured up lazy summer days and gentle, restful summer nights.

And the house . . .

She had discovered that childhood memories were often diminished by an adult's perspective, but not on this occasion. In the early evening light the house looked mysteriously untouched by time. She might have been eight years old again, carefree and giggling, as she ran in and out of the latticed archways that were off to the side of the house and that dripped with wisteria the color of dark lilac.

The house was large and rambling with a gabled roof punctuated by numerous chimneys. A deep, shaded porch ambled along its width and around one side. At the corner it circled outward to accommodate a table and chairs, this portion topped by a turret roof. A tower that climbed three stories was at the other end of the house. On the second floor there was a recessed porch that could be reached through tall French windows that opened outward from a large bedroom. Delicate, beaded spindle-work frieze was suspended from the ceiling of both porches, and lacy spandrels decorated every right angle. The house looked like a multitiered cake, iced and decorated, waiting for the party to begin.

But she knew the party was over and had been for many years.

A persistent beeping sound jolted her from her reverie. With a sigh for an enchanted time that would never come again, she glanced at her watch, then pushed the button that would stop the alarm. Four minutes had passed since she had arrived; she could hardly believe it. It wasn't like her to let time slip away like that, but then it wasn't every day that she revisited a place she hadn't seen for twenty years.

Remembering the alarm and what it signaled, she leaned through the car window, grabbed her black leather Chanel purse off the car seat, pulled an antacid bottle from its depths, and popped two of the tablets into her mouth. Then she slung the purse's gold chain over her shoulder and jogged up the steps to the front door.

Peering through the screen door, she couldn't see anyone, but she could hear a scraping sound that indicated someone was working inside. She jabbed the doorbell while twirling a long, tightly curled tendril of hair with a finger. Early this morning before the sun was up and before she had set out from Dallas, she had ruthlessly pulled back her hair into a ponytail, but now it felt as if at least half of it had escaped its confinement. The thought bothered her very little.

She jabbed at the doorbell again and noticed what she hadn't from the car. The house paint was cracked and peeling. While she waited for someone to answer the door, she flicked at the peeling paint with a short, unpolished nail. When she had cleaned a narrow path around the doorbell down to the wood, she looked at her watch again. Darn it, she was wasting time, and she *hated* to waste time. She needed to phone Sam to see how the meeting on the Fort Worth car dealership had gone, then check into renting a trailer. And so far the antacids weren't helping the pain in her stomach. She should definitely think about getting something to eat.

"Hello?" she called, opening the screen door and entering the house.

She followed the scraping sound to the dining room. A man stood on a stepladder, his back to her, scraping paint from the molding. He was barefoot and whistling tonelessly.

She came to a dead stop; her mouth dropped open.

The tight jeans and T-shirt he wore revealed a body that made her mind race and her heart beat faster. And his buttocks—well, any woman would stare, she told herself. They were tightly muscled and their enticing shape cried out for a woman's hands. Surprisingly she felt her palms dampen.

She pulled herself up short, shut her mouth, and reminded herself her survey was strictly professional. And *in* her professional opinion he had a lower body *made* for a jeans commercial and an upper torso that could sell more T-shirts than Marlon Brando had when he appeared in *The Wild One* in the fifties and taught everyone that T-shirts could be worn as an outer garment. The man on the ladder was wasting his time scraping old paint from moldings. He could make a fortune as a model. She wondered if he had an agent and made a mental note to find out.

"Excuse me, but could you help me?"

Cameron Tate jerked around, and his eyes widened at the young woman who stood there, breaking the quiet and the peace of the evening not by her voice but by her very presence. If she had materialized before his eyes, molecule by molecule, he couldn't have been more astounded. In the Victorian dining room she was an extraordinary anomaly.

She was wearing a pair of ancient cutoffs that showed off long legs and trim thighs and a sleeveless, scooped-neck T-shirt that at one time might have been blue, but was now a shade of gray. Completing her outfit were a pair of beat-up tennis shoes—no socks—and an expensive-looking purse. But her attire wasn't what had riveted his attention.

It was *her* and the curious way his heart and body had instantly responded to her.

She had green eyes that shimmered like a deep lake, honey-colored skin that gleamed with soft allure, and a wild mass of red ginger hair that made him want to see just how messed up he would have it after hours of making love to her.

She smiled. "Hi, I'm Mel Lanier. I'm sorry I startled you, but I did ring the bell."

"Your name's Mel?"

She was having a hard time not staring, so as quickly as possible, she tried to make a tally of his attributes, just as she would anyone she were considering for a modeling job. Her work had always made her feel safe, and at this moment she badly needed to feel safe.

His thick ash-brown hair didn't seem to be

combed into any recognizable style. In fact its slightly longer-than-normal length suggested that it had been a while since he had bothered going to a barbershop. And the strong, rugged features that formed his face weren't at all good-looking in the conventional, male model sort of way she was used to seeing everyday in her work. But she was willing to bet *GQ* would sell out if he appeared on its cover, and it wouldn't be the men who would be doing the buying.

He had a masculinity that made everything feminine in her tingle. Just looking at him made her think of sex. And not the kind of sex in which she had participated a grand total of two times when she had been in college, the kind that had consisted of furtive groping and very little satisfaction. No, the kind of sex this man made her think of was the kind she tried to evoke every day to sell all kinds of products, no matter what they were. The kind of sex that conjured up images of bewitchment, enchantment, obsession, and, most of all, unimaginable pleasure.

And as if that wasn't enough, he also had the penetrating blue eyes of Paul Newman. This man, she concluded, could sell anything from banks to cars to refrigerators, and she, along with every other woman in America, would buy.

She suddenly realized he was looking at her strangely, no doubt waiting for her to answer. "Actually my full name is Melisande, but everyone calls me Mel."

He wiped the scraper he had been used on a rag and fixed her with his piercing eyes. "Melisande is an unusual name."

"Yes, yes it is." Her name always drew comment, and for that reason she never mentioned it unless asked. "I'm looking for Cameron Tate.

Could you tell me where I could find him?" Thinking that if he knew the time, he could put it together with the schedule of the new owner of the house and be able to figure out his whereabouts, she glanced at her watch and added, "It's seven fifty-one."

He climbed down the stepladder. "Who was the romantic who named you Melisande? Your mother or your father?"

Impatience was a familiar emotion to her. She had had to learn that not everyone was as driven as she was, so she kept her voice even as she answered. "My mother."

"Your father wasn't a romantic?"

Her father had been a drunk, but she had never told anyone that, and she wasn't about to start with this man just because he had eyes that made a woman contemplate what it would be like to go to bed with him. She infused her voice with a politeness that carried an undeniable portion of steel. "It would really be helpful if you could tell me where I can find Mr. Tate at this time of day." She again glanced at her watch and informed him, "It's seven fifty-two." She couldn't resist the urge to add "and twenty-two seconds," and was annoyed at herself. After the lecture she had received from her doctor the day before yesterday, she was trying her best to improve.

"You know to the second what time it is?"

He seemed to find that odd, and her answer was unintentionally defensive. "It's not hard. All you need is a watch." Hers was a digital and a brand she had found to be more accurate than most. "Now, can you tell me—?"

He walked slowly to her, and the closer he drew, the more prominent the dusting of freckles over her nose and cheeks became. Delightful, he thought.

But the shadows beneath her eyes . . . where had those come from? "Did Phyllis send you?"

The minute he asked the question, he knew the answer. In the procession of women friends his sister had paraded before him in the last few weeks, none of them had come close to resembling this woman—this Melisande—who had appeared out of the twilight. The other women had all been perfect and dainty pastel rosebuds, blue-blooded Southern princesses to the tips of their perfectly manicured nails.

But Melisande was a vivid, sensual, scarlet rose in full bloom, and he was surprised to find he wanted to pick her.

She shook her head. "I'm sorry, but I don't know a Phyllis."

His eyes roved freely and openly over her. "Melisande is a lovely name. It conjures up a mystic, enigmatic romanticism not often found in this world. You shouldn't shorten it."

She had never been slow with a retort, but she found herself having to pause before she answered in order to give herself time to gather her thoughts. She supposed it was his eyes that were throwing her. They were the eyes of a man who didn't miss anything and, she was willing to bet, sometimes saw more than people wanted him to. She didn't know what he did for a living, but she was positive he didn't spend all his time scraping paint.

"By the way," he said, "the doorbell doesn't work."

"Oh." Suddenly she was very aware of her skin and the nerves that lay beneath.

"You're not from around here, are you?"

"No." He nodded as if she had given him the

answer he expected. She added, "I live in Dallas. Listen . . . do you even know Cameron Tate?"

He wasn't deliberately evading her questions. It was just that his own questions and her answers were so much more interesting to him. "What are you doing here in Lacy? It's off the major highway, and that pretty much makes it an out-of-the-way place."

She was clenching her jaw, she realized, and forced herself to relax. "I'm *looking* for Mr. Tate."

The muscle moving along her jaw line drew his attention. He would learn nothing more until she got her answer. "Then this is my lucky day," he drawled in a dark, husky voice that sounded as if he had heated molasses curling around his tongue.

Her mouth fell open. Again. "*You're* Cameron Tate? Why didn't you tell me?"

"I think I just did." His gaze dropped to her lips. "What can I do for you, Melisande?"

She was rarely flustered. Remaining cool under pressure was one of her trademarks. And she wasn't flustered now, she reassured herself. Everything was going to be fine. This was a simple matter. After all, supply and demand was the foundation of business. And he had something she wanted, and she was willing to pay for it. "You can sell me your bed."

Sparks of humor appeared in his eyes. "This is getting more and more interesting. I own quite a few beds, Melisande. Could you be more specific?"

She didn't even let the fact that he had called her by her full name bother her. And although it was amazingly tempting, she also didn't allow herself to wonder just how many beds he did own, and to what purpose he put them. Her goal was in sight, and as was her way, she went straight for it.

"It's the big cherry-wood, four-poster with the wonderful mattress that belonged to the previous owner of this house, Sarah St. Jerome. It's in the large bedroom on the second floor at the front of the house, the one that was her bedroom."

He nodded. "That's the bedroom I'm using now."

"Good, then you know exactly what I'm talking about."

He didn't have a clue. What's more, he didn't think he cared. Thoughts and emotions swirled in his head, the prime one being fascination. He knew that Melisande might fall well short of what Phyllis wanted for him, but his tightening muscles told him she might be exactly what he wanted. "I know which bed you're talking about. It's the bed I sleep in."

"It's a wonderful bed, isn't it?"

"I have no complaints."

He hadn't moved, his tone of voice hadn't changed, but all at once, she felt as though she were walking through a mine field, and she wasn't sure why. She was in a place where she had spent a short, but extremely happy period of time. She shouldn't be feeling this tingling and rasping of nerves. "You've already said you have other beds, so there really shouldn't be a problem. Now, I know you must be busy, and I don't want to take any more of your time than is necessary, so if you'll just name your price, I'll write you a check, make the plans to pick it up, and be on my way."

The matter settled as far as she was concerned, she glanced around the empty room, her mind, as it was most of the time, in racing gear. She lived her life at supersonic speed, and she could easily juggle three phone calls at once while laying out an ad campaign. It was no wonder this transaction was making her tense; it seemed to be taking an inordinate amount of time.

His blue eyes stayed on her, and she wondered what he was thinking. The silence stretched until she felt compelled to break it.

"Look, if I could just check your yellow pages, I'll find out where the nearest place is to get a trailer. With luck I can be back on the road by"—she glanced at her watch—"nine-thirty, nine thirty-five at the latest. Are you going to strip this wallpaper too? It's a shame to lose it, but it is in pretty bad shape." She was accustomed to switching quickly from one idea to another, but she had the irritating feeling that this switch had been strictly self-defensive. "You could probably find a print that's close to this one." She leaned closer and picked at a hole with her nail. "Or there are places that can reproduce the print for you." She knew this because she had once done an ad campaign for a company who did just that. "It would cost quite a bit, but the result would be really wonderful. On the other hand, there are some lovely prints available that would be quite reasonable. It just depends on what you want to spend."

He tilted his head to one side, but no matter the angle, the view was just as spectacular. She wasn't beautiful in the way Phyllis and her friends were. And she seemed to have a thing about her watch. But he had the funny, intriguing feeling that he had just lost something. Like any chance of keeping his heart whole and to himself.

She looked at him and gently reminded, "Yellow pages?"

"Would you like a cup of coffee?"

She shook her head. "I never drink caffeine."

It was a good thing, he thought, amused. She

was already as tightly wound as her marvelous hair. "In that case I think I saw some herbal tea in the pantry. Apparently Sarah was a tea drinker."

Twinkling blue lights danced in his eyes. It wasn't as if she had never seen eyes twinkle. She had. But . . .

She nodded absently, thinking that he had the most interesting eyes she had ever seen. Then she realized that she had just agreed to have a cup of tea with him. She shook her head hard, sending her curls flying. "Thank you, but I don't really have the time."

She raised her wrist to take yet another look at her watch, but to her amazement, he closed his hand around her arm, and before she knew what was happening, he was guiding her into the kitchen.

"I know. You have to be on the road by nine thirty-five at the latest, but I think you're going to have a problem meeting that schedule."

His touch did unsettling things to her nervous system and made her feel light-headed. As much as she hated to agree with the doctor, maybe she *was* on the verge of being very ill. "Why?"

"Well, for one thing, there aren't any places close by that I know of where you can get a trailer." He released her arm when he reached the pantry. "You'll probably have to go into the next town, but even then they won't be open this late. Not much is."

She had considered that this might be the case and with reluctance had come prepared to spend the night. She was a realist, and though she would have much preferred to go back home tonight, she also knew that her overstrained eyes could use the rest. But she wasn't looking forward to staying over. For the past year or so she hadn't been able to sleep well, even in her own home. She knew she would never be able to sleep in a strange place and a strange room where probably ten-thousand-plus strangers had slept before her.

Once she had Aunt Sarah's bed, though, her insomnia would disappear. One or two more nights without sleep weren't going to kill her. "Then I'll just have to check into a motel. I saw one not too far from here."

He smiled. "You could stay here."

For one demented moment she actually considered his invitation, and her opinion was split as to whether it was because of him or the bed. "You mean I could sleep in the cherry-wood bed?"

The twinkling increased. "Sure, you could. But as I said, that's where I sleep."

She stared at him. Had he just propositioned her? Strangely enough she didn't find the idea nearly as ridiculous or offensive as she should have. She must be even more tired than she thought.

He held a package of tea toward her. "Is this all right?"

"Perfect." Grateful for something to do, she snatched it from him and scooped up the teakettle from the stove. She crossed to the sink and filled the teakettle, then returned to the stove. Staring into the fire that burned beneath the kettle, she thought of his eyes. *Dammit*. "Maybe there's someone around here who has a pickup and would like to make some extra money taking the bed back to Dallas for me." She glanced over her shoulder at him. "Do you know of anyone?"

"Dallas?" He shook his head. "That's a long trip. Did you drive all the way from there today?"

"Yes," she said, spying the coffeepot. "How old

is that coffee? Do you want me to make a new pot for you?"

"No, it's fine. Why are you so determined to go back tonight? You must be exhausted."

She shrugged, absently rubbing her stomach and the vague pain there. "Just a little tired, but then I'm always tired."

He found it hard to believe she could ever be tired. He could almost see the sparks of energy emanating from her. "You know what? I'm starved. How about you?"

Maybe food *would* help, she thought. She had promised the doctor to try to eat more regularly, but other than a piece of leftover pizza of uncertain age she had found in the refrigerator this morning she hadn't had anything else all day. And besides, eating with him wouldn't be wasting time, she rationalized, because during the meal she could press him to name his price. She frowned, wondering why she felt the need to justify spending more time with him. She wheeled for the refrigerator. "What do you have to eat?"

He caught her arm and gently guided her to a chair at the kitchen table. "Sit down. You're my guest, and I'll make us dinner."

"Are you sure you don't want me to help?"

"Positive."

She felt better when she was busy. But, she reminded herself, she wanted something from him and she should try to be a good guest.

The kitchen was a large room, with all the cabinets, counters, and cupboards at one end, and an oblong oak table at the other. The matching chairs had faded chintz cushions tied to them with neat little bows, and the chintz matched the curtains that lazily drifted at the open windows.

"Do you cook?" she asked in an attempt at

small talk. It was something she had never been good at, and watching him bend over and peer into the refrigerator, she quickly forgot her attempt. Lord, he had a posterior *made* for a pinup poster.

He pulled out several covered bowls and plates and set them on the drainboard. "On occasion, but I won't have to tonight. Today at noon Elizabeth Cole brought over a ham, potato salad, baked beans, and homemade bread. I'll heat it all up for us."

"Who's Elizabeth Cole?" she asked, hard-pressed to tear her gaze from him as he moved around the kitchen. Even his bare toes were sexy. If she hired him to pose for a jeans commercial, she'd have the caption beneath his picture read:

> *Ladies, wouldn't you just love to chew the buttons off his button-fly jeans? Buy him a pair and have at it.*

"Elizabeth is one of my sister's, friends. Ever since I've been here, Phyllis has made it her mission in life to find me a suitable bride."

"Bride?" She felt a sharp, stabbing pain in her stomach. There was a basket of pink, lavender, and blue paper napkins in the center of the table. She grabbed the pile and began neatly sorting them by color. "Do you want to get married?" she asked casually.

"Sure. When and if the right person comes along." He punched a series of buttons on a microwave that looked brand-new, and it hummed to life. "But Phyllis's choices are pretty far off the mark. So far, no bull's-eye."

"I don't know," she said, making a real effort to be fair. "Someone who can bake bread from scratch sounds as if she might make a good prospect. Have you been out with this Elizabeth?"

"Nope."

"Why not? Is she ugly?" Poor Elizabeth, she thought as she folded the napkins into triangles. She was probably one of those Southern-belle spinsters who had bad skin and wore glasses as thick as Coke bottles and shirtwaist dresses that looked like her mother's. She wasn't going to be in town long, but if she happened to meet Elizabeth, she might suggest a makeover—"

"No, she's actually very attractive."

"Oh." To hell with Elizabeth, she decided uncharitably. The woman obviously didn't need her sympathy or her suggestions.

"But if I took out every lady my sister has brought by here, I'd never finish renovating this house."

Sooner or later, though, he'd probably get around to taking out the culinarily inclined, not-to-mention attractive Elizabeth, she thought, strangely glum. She replaced the folded napkins in the basket at interesting angles that drew the eye. That done, she glanced around, searching for something else she could do. "Restoring a house this size is a big job. Have you told your sister to stop bringing her friends around?"

"I've told her, but it hasn't stopped her, and since she's at a point in her life where she needs a distraction, I let her do it. It's a relatively harmless pastime."

"Maybe to you, but what about the women? I'm sure they would love to marry you." She could imagine the pain a woman might feel if she allowed herself to get her hopes up about him, then have those hopes dashed.

He skewered her with a sharp gaze. "Why would you say that?"

She had no idea. "Just a guess."

"Anyway I never give then any encouragement."

"Just having you look at them could give them encouragement," she muttered.

"What?"

"Nothing." She was shocked. She was actually reacting to him as a man. She tried to remember the last time it had happened and couldn't. A man was either a client; an employee; a friend's husband, boyfriend, or brother; or a means to sell a product. Up to this point she had tried to lump him with the latter group. So far she hadn't been what she would call really successful.

He placed a cup of hot herbal tea in front of her, along with a glass of water, then bent toward her and clamped his hands over hers, stopping her in the middle of aligning the salt and pepper shakers in a straight line on either side of the basket. "Don't you ever keep still?"

Her eyes locked with his. His lashes were thick, she noticed absently, and he smelled of everything elementally male—musk, earthiness, desire. . . . Or was it her own desire she smelled? She swallowed against a newly formed lump in her throat. "I'm use to working sixteen-hour days. It's hard for me to sit and do nothing." It was true, but in this particular instance she had the uneasy suspicion that her need for activity could be directly ascribed to him.

"Drink your tea," he said softly. "That will give you something to do."

Willing to agree to anything that would get the force of his attention off her, she nodded in acquiescence.

But he didn't immediately straighten away. Instead he lifted a hand to a long, corkscrew tendril that lay by the side of her face and fingered the tightness of the curl and the silkiness of its texture. "Is this a permanent?"

She refused to give him even a small indication of what his nearness was doing to her, how it had heat winding through her lower abdomen and her breath sticking in her lungs. "That's a very rude question. It's like asking a woman if her hair color is real."

He slowly smiled. "I already know your hair color is real, Melisande—it couldn't be anything else—and my guess is so are these curls."

"My name is Mel. And believe me, if a hairdresser had done this to my hair, I would sue."

His smile broadened. "If I was on the jury, you wouldn't get a cent. I think your hair is beautiful. And as for your name, it's Melisande. You told me so yourself." He straightened away from her and returned to the stove.

He had said her hair was beautiful, she thought, a warm glow spreading through her. His compliment shouldn't have such a potent effect on her, but much to her chagrin she found it did. This was a man she hadn't even known until—she checked her watch—forty-two minutes ago. And she would never see him again after she picked up the bed in the morning. Yet he had her heart beating like a drum. How ridiculous. His effect on her must have something to do with the perfumed air. The air in Dallas was perfumed, but with vigor, energy, and ambition. Here it was with . . . romance and sensuality. If she had the time, she might suggest to the chamber of commerce that they bottle the air and sell it at a nice little profit.

She watched him as he prepared dinner, moving around the kitchen with an efficiency she admired and a male grace she found mesmerizing.

In a matter of minutes he returned to the table with a basket of hot bread and sat it before her. The aroma had her mouth watering.

"Help yourself. Everything else will be ready in just a little while."

She immediately took a piece of bread and was reminded of the bread her great-aunt Sarah had made for her the summer she had stayed here. "This is *fabulous*."

"Elizabeth is a wonderful cook."

Her enthusiasm dropped. "She sounds a veritable treasure. You should snap her up before she gets away." Fortunately the bread in her mouth lessened the impact of her sarcasm.

He walked back to the stove. "So what do you do for sixteen hours a day, Melisande?"

"I own an ad agency."

"Really? Where's your office?"

"Are you familiar with the Dallas area?"

"Yes."

"Well, my office is in the North Dallas area. The location gives me access to downtown Dallas, Las Colinas, and even Fort Worth." She took a sip of her tea and eyed him consideringly. "What about you? Are you a model by any chance?"

He broke out laughing. "No, that's too much work."

"Then what do you do?"

"Only things that I love, and even then as little as I can get away with."

She didn't buy it. Somehow he didn't seem the kind of man to be content with lying on a couch in front of a television drinking beer all day. "Restoring houses is hard work."

"Yes, it is, but I'm having a good time, and that's

what's important. Besides, I'm not doing it alone. I have help—my workers have gone home for the night. And I've always loved this house. I was raised here in Lacy, and I rode my bicycle by here several times a week. When I heard the St. Jerome heirs were selling it, furniture and all, I immediately made an offer."

She nodded. "I wish I had known. I would have made an offer, but I wasn't told."

His expression turned curious. "Is there some reason you should have been?"

"No, not really. Sarah St. Jerome was my great-aunt, but I'm on an obscure branch of the family tree. And to be truthful, I really couldn't use the house. If it were located in Dallas, it would be a different matter, but it's not, and it would be hard for me to come here on a regular basis.

"But you said you would have made an offer."

"For the bed." At his blank look she added, "The cherry-wood bed, the one that's in my great-aunt Sarah's former bedroom, the one that I'm buying."

Staring into her green eyes, he realized that he had momentarily forgotten why she was here. He placed a plate in front of her, generously heaped with food, and one in front of himself and sat down across from her. But instead of eating, he propped his elbows on the table and clasped his hands together.

"Tell me something," he said slowly. "Is there something I've missed here? Because, you know, it's funny, I don't remember putting the bed up for sale."

"But you will, won't you? I mean, the bed means nothing to you."

He considered the pucker lines of worry between her brow, then met her gaze. "How do you know it doesn't?"

He certainly had her there. She had considered that he might not have *thought* of selling the bed, but for some reason she had never considered that he might not *want* to sell the bed. It was another example of her tunnel vision. When she became fixated on a certain goal, she didn't bother looking right or left. She just marched straight ahead until she reached that goal. "*Does* the bed mean something to you?"

"I've grown to like it."

Ignoring the hunger and the pains in her stomach, she shoved her plate away. "Yes, but it can't really *mean* anything to you. Not like it does to me."

"Suppose you tell me exactly what it does mean to you."

She eyed him assessingly, wondering if artful elaboration would help her. It worked with everything else she sold.

He grinned. "Is this going to be fiction or fact, Melisande?"

It was those eyes. He saw everything. But she met his gaze straight on. "Which do you want it to be?"

"Try fact. If it doesn't work, you can always go back to fiction."

Good idea, she thought. "The truth is that I once spent part of a summer here when I was eight years old. Aunt Sarah let me sleep in her bed during that time, and I would like to have the bed to remind me of her and that wonderful summer."

It was only part of the truth, he thought, though he didn't know how he knew it. "That's not all, is it?"

Her frustration level was climbing. "Is it just me, or do you see through everyone?"

He slowly smiled. "There's something about you, Melisande, I can't deny it."

She was pretty shrewd herself, and she knew a danger sign when she saw one. There was no way she was going to ask him what he had meant. "Okay, here it is. I slept like a rock in Aunt Sarah's bed that summer. In fact it's about the last time I slept even half as well, and since I've been having a little trouble sleeping lately, I—"

"How much trouble?"

She shifted uneasily. It was hard for her to admit something she considered a weakness, even to herself. "Some."

"Some," he repeated thoughtfully, his gaze on the shadows beneath her eyes. "I see, and you decided the bed was the answer to your insomnia?"

"I *know* it is. At any rate my buying the bed can't be that big a deal to you. My second cousin, Alicia St. Jerome, told me that you've owned the house and the bed only a couple of months. Did you move in immediately?"

"No. I've been staying here just about a month."

She smiled triumphantly. "There you are, then. You can't have grown that fond of the bed in that length of time."

"It's only two weeks' less time than you had with the bed."

She was clenching her jaw, she realized, but she couldn't seem to stop. "Yes, but that's different. To most people a bed is a bed is a bed, and you probably sleep like a log."

"As a matter of fact I do."

"Good, then, name your price."

"There is no price."

"There's got to be," she said, desperation tingeing her voice. She had been so sure the answer to her problem was within her grasp.

He shook his head. "No. I agreed to buy the house and everything in it because I thought the furnishings went perfectly with the house. The heirs took a few pieces, but they left everything else, and I like it all exactly where it is."

She looked at him, perplexed. "You can't just say no like that."

"I can't?"

Dammit, his eyes were twinkling again. Why? What did he know that she didn't? "At least say you'll think about it."

He started to speak, then stopped himself. After a moment's consideration, he said, "All right, Melisande. I'll think about it. Does that make you happy?"

"It makes me happier than I was a few seconds ago, but—"

"Consider it a start, and in the meantime eat." He pushed her plate toward her.

His concession was something, she told herself, and it was much better than a definite no. She still had a chance, and she would have to be satisfied with that for now. "All right. I'll drop the subject for tonight, but I'll be back in the morning."

He smiled. "I'll be looking forward to it."

Two

The motel sat back from the road and consisted of ten units, with carports separating each unit from the other. Melisande viewed the setup as a good sign that the cabin she would be given would be quiet.

An older man who introduced himself as George Whitmark showed her to Cabin 1. "Newly decorated," he said proudly. He was tall and lanky, with a thin cover of gray hair over his head. "How do you like it?"

She took in the beige carpet and the beige bedspread that matched the beige curtains. Bland, she mentally pronounced. "Very nice," she said, then got down to what was really important to her. "What kind of mattress is on the bed?" She crossed the room and sat down on the bed, though she knew sitting was no test.

He beamed. "It's brand-new. Orthopedic. I'm upgrading the place, one cabin at a time. I've done One and Two, and now I'm working on Three."

The mattress would be hard as a board, she thought with resignation, but it wouldn't matter

23

anyway. She wouldn't sleep but a short while; she never did. "Thank you very much, Mr. Whitmark."

"George. Just call me George. Everyone does. And if you need anything at all, just pick up the phone."

With a smile she saw him to the door, then unloaded the station wagon. Once she had everything she had brought with her inside, she stripped the bed, laid down her own egg-crate mattress pad over the new mattress, remade the bed with her own sheets, and then added her own pillow. Next she plugged in her sleep machine and placed it on the nightstand. It was the most expensive sleep machine on the market, and it emitted a hypnotic white sound that was supposed to mask noises and soothe its user to sleep.

Yeah, right, she thought sourly as she went into the bathroom, drew a tubful of water, and poured in some scented bath oil. The sleep machine's literature boasted of a high percentage of success, but so far, with her, it had proved to be a complete failure. But she always turned it on, ever hopeful. It was part of the ritual she went through each and every night.

The relaxing bath was also part of that ritual. The problem was, the bath never relaxed her. She had always found lying in a tub of hot water incredibly boring and a huge waste of time, and tonight she seemed to be wound tighter than usual. She bolted from the tub. A glance at her watch told her she had lasted five minutes and two seconds.

"I don't care what the so-called sleep experts say," she muttered, slipping into the oversized sleep shirt that she had washed so often it had become as soft as her own skin, "I'm not taking any more baths."

She climbed into the bed, using the left side, as was her habit, took off her watch and put it on the bedside table beside her, turned out the lights, and dutifully shut her eyes.

And the expected happened. Sleep didn't come.

Then the unexpected happened. Unbidden, Cameron appeared in her mind. Cameron with his blue eyes that could convince a woman to do anything and that smile that could break a heart. He had seemed perfectly at ease heating up one woman's cooking for another. Maybe Elizabeth did deserve her sympathy after all.

What would it be like for a woman if she allowed herself to fall in love with him? she wondered. She might lose herself forever in the depths of his eyes and get a great deal of pleasure in the bargain. In short Cameron Tate was the worst sort of trap, the kind of trap one might walk willingly into without a backward glance. And just who was he anyway? He owned Aunt Sarah's house, and he had said he was enjoying renovating it. But Melisande didn't have any idea what he did for a living, or if he did anything, though she had asked. He had said he only did things that he loved, and even then as little as possible. She hadn't bought it, but she hadn't pressed either. And she knew why.

She didn't want to know too much about him.

She didn't want him to stay in her mind after she returned to Dallas. She didn't want to wonder what he was doing with the house. Or with Elizabeth. Or with any of the other candidates-for-wife his sister brought over.

She hadn't liked the way he made her feel—vaguely needy, vaguely achy. And she hadn't liked the things that had gone through her mind as she had sat there in the kitchen and watched him.

With a sound that came close to despair, she

rolled over onto her stomach and punched the pillow. She had to stop thinking about him. She had to get some sleep.

And toward dawn, she did fall asleep, but as usual, her sleep was fitful, and she didn't awake rested.

The alarm on her watch went off promptly at seven. Automatically her hand shot out, found the watch on the bedside table, and pressed the button to stop the ringing sound. With a groan she rolled out of bed. No matter how little sleep she had had the night before, she always got up at the same time every morning. It was another credo put out by sleep experts, but she would have done it anyway. A person couldn't sleep the morning away and expect to get anything done.

In the bathroom she stepped beneath a briskly running shower, lathered her hair, then let the water rain down on her head, waking her up and rinsing her hair at the same time. She loved showers. They were efficient and energizing, two things of which she wholeheartedly approved.

Back in the bedroom, she delved through the overnight bag she had brought and pulled out a pair of jeans and a green silk blouse.

She frowned at the blouse and the tiny red tag sewed inside the collar. The red tag meant that the blouse went only with other articles of clothing that also had similar red tags, and, just her luck, she hadn't brought a single other red-tag item with her. Her mind had always been too fixated on achieving success in her work to give much thought to clothes. She was totally disinterested in what went with what and what looked good on her. But when she had started her own business, she had known that she needed to dress for success. So one day she had walked into an exclusive boutique owned by the bright and beautiful Noelle Durrell and thrown herself on the woman's mercy.

In a blink of an eye Noelle had put together a perfectly coordinated mix-and-match wardrobe for her. And to make certain she always knew what went with what, Noelle had sewn tags of different colors into all the garments. All the blue tags could be worn together, as could all the yellow tags, and so on. Noelle called it "Garanimals for Mel."

Melisande's frown deepened. She distinctly remembered Noelle telling her she could wear just about any top with her jeans, but she didn't want to wear the silk blouse. She would be traveling all day, and she needed to wear something she wouldn't have to worry about getting dirty.

She delved through the bag, and with a triumphant sound pulled out a plain white T-shirt. She quickly dressed and worked styling gel through her thick, wet curls. Not wanting to take the time to strip the bed properly, one item at a time, she simply threw the pillow in the middle, then started at the bottom and rolled her sheet, egg-crate mattress pad, and pillow into a huge bedroll, then remade the bed with George Whitmark's bed linen.

She threw the rest of her things into the bag, took two antacid tablets, and headed out the door to her car.

The new day had brought her a new sense of purpose and resolve. Cameron was going to sell her Aunt Sarah's cherry-wood bed. He *had* to. And then she was going to leave this place with its perfumed air and go back to Dallas, where she belonged.

"You're not leaving today, are you?" George called, pausing outside Cabin 3.

Melisande gave him a smile. "Yes, I am. I need to get back to Dallas, but I really enjoyed my stay." It wasn't exactly the truth, but she saw no reason to burden him with talk of her insomnia, not to mention her preoccupation with a certain blue-eyed man.

"Well, you come back anytime, you hear?" With a wave he disappeared into Cabin 3.

"Good morning, Sam," Melisande said into her car phone as soon as her art director came on the line.

"Hey, Mel. How are things over there in Alabama?"

"Tremendous," she said with dry irony, "just tremendous." She rarely shared her feelings with anyone, but Sam was one of the exceptions. He had been with her since she started her company, and she was very close to him. But even if she had been inclined to share her feelings now, she wouldn't know how. She didn't even know how to share them with herself. Where Cameron Tate was concerned, her mind refused to process information logically.

Only one thought kept her from panicking: Once she got away from this place and returned home, her head would clear.

"I'm on my way back to Aunt Sarah's house. I plan on closing the deal on the bed, arranging for its transportation, then hitting the road, all in short order. I should be back in the office tomorrow morning, no problem."

"Mel . . ." Sam's put-out tone came through

loud and clear. "The doctor said you needed a vacation."

"Well, he's wrong. All I need is a good night's sleep. Now tell me how your meeting with the automobile dealership went. I meant to call you last night, but by the time I got to the motel, I decided it was too late." Sam was one of those disgusting people who cheerfully fell asleep promptly at ten every night. "Did they go for our package?"

"Lock, stock, and barrel."

"Great! And they weren't upset that I wasn't there?"

"Not at all. I explained you had a family emergency, but that you had overseen every detail of the layout yourself and that as soon as you got back, you would drive over—for that all-important personal touch, don'tcha know—to make sure they were entirely happy. And in the meantime, those of us in the office were perfectly capable of getting the campaign under way immediately."

"Good. Good." She had been worried about Sam making the presentation. He was brilliant, but with his long, ponytailed hair, artistic-looking round glasses, and regulation uniform of blue jeans and T-shirt, he sometimes put people off.

She had always been very comfortable with him, though. His eyes weren't piercing, and he didn't overwhelm her with a virility so strong, he made her aware of her heartbeat and breathing pattern.

"Mel, are you there?"

"Yes. Sorry. My mind wandered."

"Do me a favor, rethink your plans. Stay for a few days."

"I can't do that, and you know it."

"At the risk of causing your psyche major trauma, I feel the strong need to point out that we could manage quite nicely without you for a couple of weeks. We need you, but we don't need you falling to pieces on us."

"There's no way I'd ever do that. I'll see you tomorrow."

From his position on the front porch Cameron eyed the approach of the battered station wagon with unmistakable pleasure.

Melisande—a mystical name, an out-of-the-ordinary woman.

He had been waiting for her.

He leaned back in the wicker rocker, stretched his long legs out in front of him, and sipped his coffee.

He knew his manner and appearance gave people who didn't know him well the impression that he was laid-back. But in reality, beneath his free-and-easy style, there was solid steel. And when he really cared about someone or something, he could be ruthless.

He wasn't sure he believed in love at first sight, but he did believe with all his heart in *fascination* at first sight. Fascination was what he had felt the minute he had laid eyes on Melisande.

He had turned around, seen her, and been transfixed.

And he did not want her to leave today. Or tomorrow.

He wanted the opportunity to get to know her better. He wanted to learn what she liked and didn't like. What made her tick. What made her smile. What made her moan with ecstasy.

As a matter of fact he wanted all those things and much more with a ferocity that shocked him.

And there was something else. He wanted to help her.

He wasn't sure why he thought she needed help or why he thought he could be the one to help her. It was just something he felt with a strength that couldn't be shaken.

The bed. She wanted the bed. What luck.

If he played his cards right, he could keep her here for a few days and maybe longer. And if that didn't work, he had one last ace up his sleeve.

Melisande slung the gold chain of her purse over her shoulder and strode up the walkway to the porch. Cameron stood as she came. He was dressed as he had been last night, in jeans and a T-shirt, and unfortunately, she reflected ruefully, he was as devastating and as stunningly virile in the daylight as he had been at twilight.

He had said he considered modeling too much work, but maybe before she left, she should try to talk him into coming to Dallas and becoming a model. He and whoever used him in their advertising campaign would make a fortune. Then again, maybe it would be best for her if there were hundreds of miles separating them.

"Good morning," he said, smiling, as she topped the last step.

"Good morning."

"Your hair's wet."

She drew a thick strand across her face so that she could see it, then let it drop. "It's always wet this time of morning. I can't blow it dry or it would expand to the size of a basketball, which is exactly what it looks like when I get up in the morning, because I have such restless nights." She shrugged. "I have to wash it every morning and let it dry in its own time. It's best."

His smile grew wider. Lord, she was enchanting.

So far there wasn't a thing he didn't like about her—except those shadows beneath her eyes. "Were you able to get any sleep?"

"Enough. Now about the bed—"

"Would you like a cup of coffee?" She hesitated. "It's decaffeinated," he added as enticement. She glanced at her watch. "Come on," he cajoled. "You can spare five minutes. Besides, I went out and bought sweet rolls and fresh fruit for us." He waved his hand toward the end of the porch, where the table was set for two, and an insulated carafe of coffee stood waiting.

It would be ungracious to refuse after he had gone to all that trouble, she reflected. And they did need to talk. Besides, she couldn't remember eating breakfast. "All right. Thank you."

The rattan table was round and had a glass top. The rattan had been glistening white the summer she had stayed here, but what paint remained had grayed.

She sat down in the seat he indicated and watched as he poured her a cup of coffee, then took the chair to her right.

Placing a pink paper napkin in her lap, one of those she had folded the evening before, she looked at him. "I hope you've thought about selling me the bed."

"I did. Sugar?"

"What?" she asked, then noticed the sugar bowl in his hand. "Oh, no, thank you. Well, what's your answer?"

"Cream?"

"Cream?" She shook her head impatiently. "No. What decision have you come to about the bed, Cameron?"

He refilled his own cup, taking his time, giving

every indication of wrestling with a weighty matter. "None," he said finally.

"None?"

"I'm sorry, but I just can't seem to make up my mind." He placed a warm coffee roll on her plate, then uncovered a small bowl of fresh strawberries.

She had had clients sit on the fence before. Secretly it made her crazy, but she had had long practice in presenting a patient, reasonable face. "Okay, let's talk about it. What element is missing that would help you make up your mind?"

"I'm not sure. You'd better eat. Your roll is going to get cold."

She popped a strawberry into her mouth, and while she was savoring its succulent flavor, she eyed him consideringly. She supposed she could sympathize with him. If the bed were hers, she would never sell it. But then her situation was different. She had something of a past with the bed, and now she needed it desperately.

"Then let's go at it from the other direction. What's *keeping* you from making up your mind?"

He forked a section of coffee roll into his mouth. After a moment he said, "Several things. For one thing, it's part of the history of the house. As I'm sure you know, Sarah and her husband moved into the house right after they were first married, and her husband had the bed specially built for them."

She nodded. "Yes, I did know that. I remember Aunt Sarah saying that it's an off size and that the mattress had to be specially made for the bed and that consequently bed linens can't be bought off the shelf."

"That's right." He pushed the roll closer to her. "Eat. I don't want it to go to waste."

Dutifully she took a bite, and because he was watching her so intently, she took another.

"I had to special-order new sheets," he said, "but I'm using one of Sarah's crocheted coverlets for the time being as a spread."

"I admit that its history is a factor," she said, torn, "but—"

"And if I decide to turn the house into a bed-and-breakfast, the bed would be a big draw."

She looked at him blankly. "You're going to turn the house into a bed-and-breakfast?"

He gave a nonchalant shrug. "I haven't completely decided yet but, yeah, maybe."

Words deserted her. Up to this point she hadn't even considered what he might do with the house, but now she found she cared. She *really* cared. She didn't much like the idea of turning the house she remembered so fondly into what would be, in effect, a hotel. But she knew more than most that things never stayed the same, and that life went forward whether you wanted it to or not.

She quickly forced herself to readjust her thinking. "People who come to stay here wouldn't miss the bed if it wasn't here, because they wouldn't know it had been here in the first place, and with the money I'll pay you for it, you can buy a magnificent four-poster."

He shook his head. "It wouldn't be the same. You're not eating."

She popped another strawberry into her mouth, and in her anxiousness to chew and swallow it quickly, she bit down too fast, causing sweet, red juice to dribble from her lips down onto her chin. With a muted sound of exasperation, she reached for her napkin, but Cameron was faster. He reached over with his finger, wiped up the juice, and then slid his finger into his mouth.

The sight made her a little breathless.

He smiled, his finger still between his lips. "Sorry, but I just couldn't help myself."

To her chagrin she couldn't tear her gaze from his lips. They were slightly reddened from the strawberry juice. And they were beautifully shaped, with the lower lip slightly fuller than the top. He could sell a million sodas simply by bringing the can to his lips and drinking. She could imagine how his lips would purse to accommodate the can, and how his throat would look as he drank—strong, tanned. . . .

And women everywhere would wish they were a soda can.

She passed a hand over her eyes. Lord, but she needed a good night's sleep.

"Are you all right?" he asked, his brow furrowed with concern.

She straightened. "Fine. Just fine. Let's see, where were we?"

"We were talking about the possibility of the house becoming a bed-and-breakfast."

"Right. Okay, I'll tell you what I'll do. I'll draw up an ad campaign for you free of charge. Using the campaign, you could have brochures made up and have them distributed to all the road clubs, plus you could advertise in some of the travel magazines. It should be a piece of cake." Because it was infinitely easier to think when she wasn't looking at him, she turned her head and gazed toward the line of oak trees and their gracefully trailing Spanish moss.

"Come to the St. Jerome house and let the magic of the South envelop you. The days glide by like satin, and the nights are a soft velvet murmur."

"That's good," he said admiringly.

She waved a dismissive hand. "It's a little trite. I

could do better if I gave it some thought. The point is, this place would be a great success as a bed-and-breakfast." She frowned at her statement.

His lips quirked. She was following him beautifully. "I agree, and the bed would be a big draw."

Her chin came up. "Not necessarily. I mean, not any more than the house itself, or its gardens."

"Then again, I may want to use the house as a second home."

"You'd keep it for yourself? This is a big place, and you're a bachelor."

"Sarah lived here alone for many years."

"She also raised a family here."

"Who's to say I won't."

She could almost see it—his giggling, happy children running in and out of the arched trellises as she had once done, climbing the trees, fishing from the riverbank. But her imagination stopped short of seeing his wife, sitting here on the porch, watching her children playing, perhaps sitting on the swing with Cameron, his arm around her.

"I guess you can see why I'm having such a hard time making a decision," he said in that warm, molasses voice of his.

She could see it, but she refused to admit it, just as she refused to accept defeat. The doctor had said all she needed to do was slow down, and her insomnia would disappear along with the preulcerous stomach pangs she had been having. But she had been going at hyperspeed for so long, she didn't know any other way to live. No, the bed was her answer, and she would not give it up easily. But what could she do?

He saw the conflicting emotions race across her face and decided it was time to make his move. "You know, if I just had a little more time to think

about it, I'm sure I could come to some decision."
Her expression turned wary, so he added a little
bait. "Who knows, I might even decide that you're
right. That the house doesn't really need the bed."

"How much time?"

"Oh, I don't know. Maybe a few days, a week at
the most."

She almost groaned. "That's a heck of a long
drive to make again at the end of the week. I'd just
about get back home and get settled and then
have to turn around and come back."

"Then stay here."

The thought sent a shock wave through her. "I
can't! There's just no way."

"Why?"

"I have a business to run, that's why."

"Surely your company can get along without
you for a few days. If it can't, you've never learned
to delegate."

It was true. She had never been able to let go of
that all-important control. She had never been
able to trust another person with anything she
really wanted. And where her business was concerned, she wanted unqualified success.

He hadn't expected this to be easy, but he was
determined. "It would be for only a few days. You
can even stay here if you like."

Stay here. With him. What would it be like to
hear that warm molasses voice of his in the middle
of the night? She shook her head, hoping to jolt
the question from her mind. "It's impossible. I
didn't even have these two days to spare."

If it hadn't been for the doctor and what he had
said, she might never even have thought of the
bed. But she had thought of it, and it offered the
perfect solution. Didn't it? Or was she pinning her
hopes on something that no longer existed as she

remembered it. After all, she hadn't seen the bed in twenty years, much less slept on it.

"Would you like to go up and see the bed?"

Her gaze turned suspicious. Those damned blue eyes of his. They would be able to beat out Superman's X-ray vision any day of the week.

"Yes, as a matter of fact I would like to see it. Things are never really what we remember, are they? I may not even want the bed once I see it again."

Dread slid along his spine at her hopeful tone. He had considered the possibility, but it was a gamble he had to take. If the gamble failed, he'd just have to think of something else to keep her here, though at the moment he had no idea what it might be.

"Are you through eating?"

She glanced down at the remains of her half-eaten sweet roll. "I'll eat the rest on the road."

"How nourishing," he muttered. She *obviously* needed help, and he was beginning to think that he was right on the mark in believing that he was the one person in the world who could help her.

Melisande stopped just inside the bedroom and let out a soft gasp. The room was of magnificent proportions, and the massive bed was its centerpiece. Its cherry-wood headboard was intricately carved, and its four posters rose nearly to the ceiling. And beneath the crocheted coverlet the mattress was thickly cushioned and padded in a way no modern mattress could ever compete with.

"It's probably smaller than you remember, right?"

For a moment she had forgotten that Cameron had followed her into the room. "No," she said quietly, "it's just as I remember it."

The hushed awe in her voice shot a thrill of victory through him, but he knew he hadn't completely won yet. He put his hand against her back and gently nudged her forward. "Go on over and look at it. Lie on it if you want."

She approached the bed with a reverence she knew was foolish. But being in this room again, seeing the bed, was bringing back things to her she had thought long forgotten. Three four-drawer walnut chests stood against one wall, exactly where she had last seen them. One long mirror with an arched top spanned their width. When Aunt Sarah had been alive, family pictures, bibelots, bits of lace, and jars of buttons had graced the top of the chest. Now there was nothing. But the light-colored marble-topped table still sat by the horsehair couch. And there was the same needlepoint rug in black, red, rose, and green on the floor at the foot of the bed. But most important, there was the bed.

She lightly trailed her fingertips across the coverlet, then closed her hand around one of the thick, smooth, cherry-wood posters. "I remember lying in this bed with Aunt Sarah that summer. She always smelled like violets, and the night air smelled like whatever the breeze happened to pick up. Some nights it was roses. Other nights it was lilacs. Some nights it was a combination." She slowly walked around the foot of the bed to the opposite side. "She would start out telling me a story, but I don't think I ever heard the end of any of them. I'd be asleep within a minute."

"I guess that made it easier for her to think up stories," he said, his voice warm with humor. "It's always easier to think of beginnings than it is to figure out a middle and an end."

She looked up, met his eyes, and smiled, sharing his humor. "I guess so."

"Don't you want to lie down? The bed might look the same, but the mattress might not be as great as you remember."

She was almost afraid to. What if it *was* as great as she remembered? What if the memories overwhelmed her and got the better of her emotions? What if it felt so good, she never wanted to get up? Then what would she do?

It wouldn't happen. She was an adult now, she reminded herself sternly. A *tired* adult, but nevertheless an adult. She could handle this.

She pulled off her tennis shoes and lay down on the bed.

Instantly her nerves soothed, her muscles loosened, her bones softened. She sank down, down, down as if she were lying on a cloud. Without being aware of what she was doing, she moaned aloud with pleasure.

Suddenly Cameron was by her side, leaning over her, staring into her eyes. "Don't make that sound again and expect to get up from this bed in the next day or two."

Shock held her still, and the fire in the depths of his blue eyes stole her breath. His easygoing manner had vanished, and in its stead, a fiery intensity burned. From the first she had had an extraordinary reaction to him, but this was the first time he had given any indication that he might be reacting to her in a similar fashion.

"I didn't mean to—"

Bewilderment was the last emotion he wanted from her. With a muttered curse he sat down beside her and put his hand on the opposite side of her body by her waist so that he was again leaning over her. Only this time his chest almost touched her breasts, and his face was within inches of hers. "I'm sorry, Melisande," he said huskily. "I should have been able to control myself a little better, but you do something to me."

Everything stopped. Her heart. Her breathing. Her mind.

She felt something happening to her, a heating of her insides, a melting of her defenses. She had no power over the sensations, and it frightened her.

"It was the mattress," she whispered. "That's all. It's just as wonderful as I remembered."

He picked up a strand of her ginger hair and fingered it. "Is it?"

She managed to nod.

"So you still want it?"

"Yes."

She wanted the bed, and he wanted her. So much so, he was actually hurting, he realized. He wanted to make her say she would stay. He wanted to taste her lips and discover the texture of the inside of her mouth. He wanted, he wanted, he wanted. . . . But instinctively he knew making any move of that sort would be a mistake.

He settled for brushing his fingers across her lips, feeling their soft fullness, then lightly tracing the outline of her bottom lip. Only when he noticed his fingers were shaking did he force himself to straighten away from her. But his hip stayed firmly against hers. "What are you going to do?" he asked brusquely.

In her wildest imaginings—and they had gotten pretty wild in the middle of last night—she had never imagined that she would be on this bed with Cameron. It was an unnervingly sensual experience, one she didn't for a minute believe she could attribute to the bed.

She pushed herself up until her back rested against the pillows and her lungs functioned more effectively. "What am *I* going to do? It's your decision, Cameron. Are you or aren't you going to sell me the bed?"

"I've already told you I need a few days."

How could such sharp eyes be so inscrutable? she wondered, both frustrated and fascinated. He might be able to read her, but she had no idea what he was thinking. "Okay, then I'll go home, and when you make up your mind, I'll hire movers to come pick up and deliver the bed."

He shook his head. "A moving company won't work."

Her brows drew together in puzzlement. "Why not?"

"First of all, I won't turn the bed over to anyone but you."

"But *I* would be hiring the movers. They would be working for me. Letting them take the bed would be exactly like turning it over to me."

"Unless you were here to personally supervise, I wouldn't let anyone touch it."

She eyed him steadily. "I think you're just being obstinate."

"Think what you like, and while you're at it, think about this. Once you leave, I'll lose the initiative to sell. Without you here to convince me, well . . ." He shrugged, leaving her to draw the obvious conclusion.

Her eyes narrowed. "Tell me the truth, Cameron. Is there even a remote possibility that you'll sell me this bed?"

His lips slowly curved into a smile. "I guess you're going to have to stay and find out."

She clenched her teeth. "I want this bed more

than I can tell you. I *need* this bed. But I can't stay away from work one more day."

He leaned toward her again and pressed the tips of his fingers against her locked jaw muscle. Slowly he began to massage the area with a circular motion, trying to ease the tension there. "You'll wear your teeth down if you don't stop doing this," he murmured huskily. "Plus it could lead to other problems, like headaches—"

His touch was one thing too many for her to contend with. With a purely reflexive, defensive movement she knocked his hand away. "Cameron, did you hear me? I *can't* stay here."

"Yes, you can. You just have to give yourself permission."

"I have to *what*?"

His eyes roamed over her, taking in the flush that tinged her freckled skin, the emotions that mixed in her lovely eyes, the shadows that lay beneath. "Don't you ever relax, Melisande?"

Somehow he seemed even closer. She caught the faint, pleasing hint of citrus. Apparently his scent was like the air, changing with the breeze and perhaps his emotions. And there was no doubt in her mind that she could make millions of dollars selling a man's cologne, *any* man's cologne, no matter what it was, if she could only distill his scent and his essence into words. "No. What I mean is, it's hard for me to relax. . . ."

He did what he told himself he shouldn't do. He did what he *had* to do. He bent and covered her mouth with his. And because he hadn't meant to kiss her, because he hadn't given himself time to think, he kissed her as he had been wanting to ever since he had first seen her, with an all-consuming, no-holds-barred, driving passion.

Any objection she might have made died in her

throat. She responded instantly and with everything that was in her. Helplessly she parted her
lips beneath his, uncaring what her action meant.
And what happened next was just as natural, just
as pleasurable. His tongue drove into her mouth
and mated with hers.

Fire spread like a storm through her lower
extremities, and a yearning and a tormented kind
of restlessness sprang full blown in her. Her
hands went to his shoulders, and her fingers
probed and clung to the muscles there. Without
knowing what she was doing, she shifted, sliding
down the pillows, drawing him with her, pushing
her fingers through the thickness of his hair.

Her response completely undid him. Levering
over her, he pressed her down into the bed with
his weight. Wanting a woman was not a new
sensation to him, but wanting a woman as much
as he did her was. His need for her affected every
cell of his body and his mind. There was no room
for anything else.

His kiss turned hotter, became more urgent.
There was no thought of restrictions or boundaries.
The feel of her full breasts and their hardened nipples thrusting against his chest tantalized and
tormented him. With a ragged sound he slipped
his hand beneath her T-shirt and encountered a
lace bra. His hand quickly delved beneath it and
took possession of her breast.

She made a soft sound of pleasure that sounded
like thunder in his ears. He kneaded the firm
mound, using a hard-fought-for gentleness that
was in sharp contrast to his demanding need for
her. And when he at last took the stiffened nipple
between his fingers, his need escalated, spiraling
and intensifying, threatening to send him over the
brink. Nothing had ever seemed as right to him,

and there was an exquisite pleasure in knowing that this was just the beginning.

His lower body was inflamed and swollen. The tightness of his jeans was killing him. Desperately needing relief, he thrust his pelvis against hers, and beneath him her hips rotated and arched in response.

She murmured his name, and he answered, "Yes, yes . . ."

Downstairs a door slammed.

"*Cam?* Are you here? *Cam?*"

He heard his name through a red-hot haze of desire. With a muttered oath he wrenched away from Melisande. Pulling air into his lungs, he turned his head toward the bedroom door. But for the life of him he couldn't think of what he should do. He only knew what he wanted to do. His body burned with wanting it.

He turned back to Melisande and saw that she looked as dazed as he felt. Her eyes were heavy lidded, her expression soft and sensual. He could have her, he thought. Right now. He could drive deep inside, and she would willingly take all of him.

"*Cam?*"

He let out an agonized groan. "Yeah, I'll be down in a minute," he called hoarsely, sitting up.

"Okay, I'll be out on the porch."

He brought an unsteady hand up to stroke Melisande's delicate cheekbone. "It's my sister. I'll go down and get rid of her."

Mutely she reached beneath her T-shirt to pull her bra over her breast. To her dismay she was shaking. Worse, her nipples burned and her entire body throbbed. A wildfire had flared up between them, she realized, and she had nearly let herself be consumed by it.

He spread his hand over her breast, and through her T-shirt felt her crazily pounding heart. "Don't cover yourself up. I didn't get to look at you, and I'm dying for a taste of you."

Raw need crawled through her bloodstream. Words lodged in her throat, preventing her from speaking. She closed her eyes.

"Are you all right?" he asked, unable to stop himself from flexing his fingers on her breast.

No, she thought. She wasn't. She couldn't believe what she had just allowed to happened, what she had encouraged. She was outraged at herself, at the way she had responded and at the way she wanted more.

She moved, scooting backward until she was once again sitting upright, and in the process dislodged his hand. She crossed her arms protectively beneath her breasts. "You shouldn't have done that. *We* shouldn't have."

"Maybe not," he said huskily, "but it was something I very badly wanted to do. I still do. How about you? What do you want?"

It was a question she couldn't face with any honesty. "I want us to keep our relationship on a business level." It was the way all her relationships were. It was the only kind of relationship she understood, the only kind she was comfortable with.

He hated her answer, but with Phyllis downstairs he knew he was going to have to accept it for now. "Does that mean we're going to have a relationship? That you're going to stay?"

"No. I don't know. I've got to think."

He had gone too far with her. His emotions had escalated beyond his control. For now, he had to back away. With fingers beneath her chin, he tilted her face upward until she met his dark, burning gaze. "I know this is really bad timing with my sister downstairs, but I want you to know something. I can't promise you I won't kiss and touch you again. It was too damned good not to do it again. And you might as well know there's more. I want to make love to you in the worst possible way. But I can promise you I will never go further than you want, and I will always protect you."

As a promise it wasn't very reassuring, because it put the responsibility squarely on her. But then that was the way she liked it. Usually.

"Stay, Melisande."

"I said I have to think about it." Lord, help her. What was there to think about? She needed to get out of here fast.

Slowly a sexy, completely disarming smile spread across his face. "It really is a great bed, isn't it?"

She looked at him. "You don't play fair at all, do you?"

"Nope." He glanced toward the door. "You might as well come downstairs with me and meet my sister and get it over with."

Nervously she thrust a hand through her hair. "I can't. I can just imagine how I must look."

"You look beautiful." His eyes began to twinkle. "Phyllis is going to love you."

Three

Cameron stepped out onto the porch and gave Phyllis a warm smile. "Morning, Sis." He glanced over his shoulder at Melisande, who was deliberately lagging behind, walking slowly down the hall, her tennis shoes in her hand. He opened the screen door wider and waited for her.

"I stopped by to tell you that—" Phyllis broke off as Melisande came out.

Cameron viewed his sister's astonished expression with humorous resignation. Her reaction was no less than he had expected. He put his arm around Melisande and drew her to him. "Phyllis, I'd like you to meet Melisande Lanier. Melisande, this is my sister, Phyllis."

Not much time had passed since Cameron had laid on top of her, devouring her mouth with his and caressing her breasts, and she hadn't recovered her equilibrium. She wasn't sure she ever would. And now his arm was around her in a possessive manner she found both alarming and exciting.

In an effort to put her feelings aside and focus

on Cameron's sister, she extended her hand. "Hi, my name's Mel."

Phyllis was lovely, Melisande thought as she grasped her hand. In comparison she felt awkward and uncomfortable. She was not only disheveled, she was wearing a pair of years-old jeans and a T-shirt, whereas Phyllis had smooth blond hair—something she had always secretly coveted—and was dressed in a buttercup-yellow sundress with matching shoes and bag. Wistfully Melisande thought of all the wonderful coordinated outfits hanging in her closet back home. If she'd only thrown in a couple of red- or even blue-tagged outfits, she could have made a better presentation.

"I thought Cameron said your name was Melisande." Phyllis was still unable to school the astonishment from her expression. And her gaze kept going back to her brother's arm around Melisande's shoulder.

"I did," he said. "Her name is Melisande."

Maybe she should have worn her green silk blouse after all, she reflected, still fretting over her appearance. At least then she would have looked a little less like a slatternly, bedraggled person who didn't know how to dress, and who, on top of everything else, had loose morals. On the other hand, she had the very sure feeling that Phyllis wouldn't approve of her no matter what she wore. She stepped out of Cameron's hold and smiled as pleasantly as she could manage. "It's Mel."

"It's Melisande," Cameron said.

Melisande shrugged. "Call me anything you want."

Phyllis looked from her to Cameron and back to her again. "Well, Melisande," she said slowly, "what are you doing here?"

Cameron pretended brotherly outrage, but he couldn't keep the laughter from his voice. "Phyllis, where are your manners?"

"I'm sorry," Phyllis said to Melisande, her expression now one of refined politeness. "I hope I didn't offend you, it's just that I thought I knew all of Cameron's friends."

"Melisande is a new friend. A very *good* friend."

Both women looked at him.

"Why don't we all go over and sit down," he said smoothly with a wave of a hand toward the table. "I'm sure there's still some hot coffee in the carafe."

Phyllis's perfectly tweezed eyebrows shot up at the sight of the table set for two. "You two were having breakfast. How *nice*." She looked back at Melisande, her wide blue eyes not as sharp as her brother's, but nevertheless impressive in their own right. "I must have interrupted."

To Melisande's ears Phyllis's pronunciation of *nice* gave the word exactly the opposite meaning—something along the lines of *immoral, unprincipled, and depraved*. "No. We had finished, and we were upstairs, uh—" She saw the trap she had set for herself and tried to escape. "We were upstairs checking out the bed." The trap closed around her. Dammit, and she was usually so good with words.

Phyllis touched her throat, a gesture that betrayed anxiousness. "You were checking out the bed?"

Cameron smiled cheerfully. "That's what she said. Would either of you like coffee?"

"No," Melisande and Phyllis said in unison.

"Which bed?" Phyllis asked.

"My bed," Cameron answered.

Phyllis's fingers tightened on her throat. "Look,

Cameron, I just stopped by to tell you that Elizabeth really enjoyed seeing you yesterday."

Cameron grinned. "Ah, yes, Elizabeth. Candidate number four. Or was she number five?"

Phyllis's eyes narrowed on her brother. "She's the fourth friend I've introduced you to. Did you like her?"

"She seemed very pleasant. By the way, tell her I really enjoyed her bread."

"It was fantastic," Melisande added, because she was once again feeling sorry for Elizabeth. How awful to be reduced to a number in Cameron's mind.

Phyllis's eyebrows once again shot skyward. "*You* had some of Elizabeth's bread?"

"Last night for dinner." Maybe it would be better if from now on she just kept her mouth shut, she reflected. Better yet she'd leave. She started edging toward the steps.

Cameron put his hand on her shoulder, stopping her. "I heated up Elizabeth's food for us. It was delicious. Be sure and tell her."

"*You* tell her," Phyllis snapped. "The whole point is to get you together with her or one of the others."

"Now, how do you suppose I could have missed that point?" he asked innocently.

She pressed manicured-tipped fingers to the middle of her brow. "Let's see . . . I also wanted to ask you if you had decided who you were going to invite to the Founders Day dance. I'm leaning toward Lisa for you."

Melisande spoke up. "I've actually grown quite fond of Elizabeth myself." She hadn't been able to help herself. It had just come out. Worse, she was having to fight the urge to laugh. When she felt the strength of two sets of blue eyes on her, she made a valiant effort to sober. "Of course I haven't had the pleasure of meeting Lisa."

Cameron's thumb began to move lightly back and forth over her shoulder. "My plans aren't definite yet, but I'm working on them."

Melisande felt heat glide down her spine, at both his touch and the soft tone of his voice, as if he were talking just to her. Thankfully, right at that moment, the alarm on her watch went off. She punched the button. "Sorry." She pulled away and hurried down to the end of the porch and the chair where she had left her purse. She was just popping a vitamin C into her mouth when Cameron strolled to the table and refilled his cup with steaming coffee from the carafe.

He looked at her. "Are you taking vitamins for any particular reason?"

"No. I've just started a new regimen to try to get healthier, and I like to stay on schedule with things." With every other thing in her life she was currently way off schedule. She felt the urgent need to regroup.

Phyllis had followed him down the porch. "The other thing I need to tell you, Cameron, is that Mary Ann is bringing dinner tonight. She makes a pecan pie that is simply heaven. You'll love it, and I think you'll like her."

"Have I met Mary Ann?"

"Yes. I introduced you the day we ran into her at the drug store."

"Oh, yeah, now I remember. Petite, bow in her hair, looked as if she would squeal at the sight of a mouse."

"She's a *lawyer*, Cameron," Phyllis said, her tone repressive, "and a very intelligent, responsible woman."

"*I* would squeal at a mouse," Melisande offered

in an attempt to defend the unknown Mary Ann. At least she would if she happened to *notice* a mouse. But for all the attention she paid to the place where she lived, she might have a whole family of mice living with her and she would never know.

"Most women would," Phyllis said, slightly mollified.

Melisande noticed Cameron eyeing her curiously. No doubt he was wondering why she felt the need to speak out for the women in the "Operation: Bride for Cameron" campaign his sister was conducting. As a matter of fact, she was also beginning to wonder. Was it a defensive move on her part? If he belonged to another woman, then maybe she wouldn't want him so much. Yeah, sure. And she might get a good night's sleep without Aunt Sarah's bed. Fat chance.

"Tell Mary Ann, thanks, but no thanks," Cameron said to Phyllis, his gaze still on Melisande. "I don't need any more food. And I have dinner plans."

"You do?" Melisande and Phyllis said in unison. Again.

"With Melisande."

She shook her head, sending her now-dry curls bouncing wildly over her head. "Not with me. You're mistaken."

He held her gaze with a compelling will. "Do we or do we not have something to discuss?"

The bed. He had her. But she refused to give in easily. "I haven't made up my mind whether or not I'm going to stay."

"Are you staying *here*?"

Phyllis's voice was higher than before, but Melisande barely noticed. She couldn't look away from Cameron and his damn blue eyes. There was something hypnotic about them.

"Yes, she is," Cameron said.

"In this house? With *you*?"

"No," Melisande said.

Cameron finally looked at his sister. "Don't you have someplace to be or something to do? Where's your husband?"

Phyllis looked at her watch, and Melisande felt an instant kinship with her. Here was someone else who could figure out where someone was by checking the time.

"It's nine-thirty. John's in his office, no doubt dictating something really important to his really important new, not to mention extremely *young*, secretary."

"Why don't you go over and invite him out for an early lunch?"

"Because I already have a lunch date and because he knows how to reach me if he wants to have lunch with me."

"What have I been telling you, Sis—?"

"I've got to go," Phyllis said, heading back to the porch steps. "It was very nice meeting you, Melisande."

Phyllis had again pronounced the word *nice* so that Melisande heard a different meaning. This time she heard *unpalatable, unpleasant, and extremely disagreeable.*

"I enjoyed meeting you, too, Phyllis, and I'm also leaving." She scooped up her purse and followed Cameron's sister, but just as she reached the steps, Cameron caught her arm.

"Stay until she's gone," he said beneath his breath. Louder, he said, "Have a nice day, Sis."

She turned on the walkway and looked back up at him. When she saw him holding Melisande's arm, she frowned. "What do you want me to tell Mary Ann? Should she wait until tomorrow night to bring dinner?"

"No. I want you to tell her and all your friends that I'm perfectly capable of cooking for myself or going out if I get hungry. I don't need this sort of 'Meals on Wheels' you've put together."

"Better think about it," Melisande said sweetly. "Phyllis said Mary Ann's pecan pie is simply heaven."

His grip on her arm tightened. "*No more,*" he said to his sister.

Phyllis's frown deepened. "Oh, all right. I'll tell Mary Ann to hold off, but you and I will talk about this again, and soon. And in the meantime be thinking about the Founders Day dance. It's just a week away, and it's important that you be there." She glanced at Melisande, then turned and gazed at the station wagon. "Is that your car?"

Melisande looked at the dust-covered, much-dented station wagon that she had bought when she had first opened her agency seven years ago. Through the windows she—and Phyllis—could plainly see the huge bedroll she had made this morning.

All the car needed was a sign in the window, saying, HAVE OWN BEDROLL, WILL MAKE HOUSE CALLS.

Next to Phyllis's sleek, shiny, smart little sports car, her station wagon looked like a den of iniquity, and a *filthy* den of iniquity at that. She started to explain that she had a very nice, late-model, *clean* sedan at home in her garage that she drove whenever she took clients out to eat, but that she hung on to the station wagon because she could carry props for photo shoots in it, plus anything else she needed. But then she decided it didn't matter. After today she would never see Phyllis again.

"Yes," she said brightly. "That's my car."

"I see."

This time Melisande didn't even bother to interpret Phyllis's tone. She simply lifted her hand and waved. "'Bye." Under her breath she said to Cameron, "So much for your sister loving me. Would you like to let go of my arm now?"

"Not particularly." Despite his words he released her. "And as for Phyllis, she's going to come to love you, trust me. But I am sorry about how she acted today. She can be a definite pain sometimes."

Melisande shrugged, her gaze on the back of Phyllis's car as it drove away. "There's nothing to apologize for. In fact I can understand why she was bothered by me. She obviously has in mind a particular type of woman for you to marry, and just as obviously I don't fit the bill."

He took her by the shoulders and turned her so that she was facing him. "It doesn't matter what Phyllis has in mind for me. When the time comes, I'll marry whoever I damn well please."

"Fine. Wonderful. Terrific," she said, infusing her tone with an enthusiasm and forcefulness she didn't entirely feel. "Just understand it doesn't concern me. By tomorrow at the latest I'm out of here."

"Then you're staying tonight?"

Sweet heaven! She had more or less said just that! "I don't know," she said, hedging. "I need to talk with my office to see if it's even possible, and then I'll have to check with George Whitmark to make sure he has a cabin I can reserve for the night.

He smiled. "He will."

His satisfied expression grated on her already overworked nerves. She pointed a stern finger at him. "Let me tell you something. If I stay—and that's *if*, you understand—you and I are going to talk, *really* talk about you selling me the bed."

"Absolutely."

She nodded, somewhat pacified that he had agreed with her. "Then I'll see you later?"

"Right. For dinner. I'll pick you up at six o'clock."

"Dinner? Oh, I don't know." Dinner sounded too much like a date to her.

"It will be a *business* dinner," he said.

Her eyes narrowed suspiciously on him. She was too good a businesswoman to believe she was that transparent.

His expression was guileless. "We've got to talk, right? And we have to eat, right? Well, dinner is about the only time I have in my schedule today to talk to you. Of course you could come back anytime today and I'd be here, but you wouldn't have my total attention, because I'd be working. In fact"—he turned his head toward the road, where he could see several cars driving toward them— "here come my workers now."

She understood schedules, and she understood the "total attention" concept. But she still couldn't help but feel that she was in some way being manipulated. The waste of her time bothered her too.

The problem was, she wanted the bed—desperately—and if one more day would help . . . Plus, dinner did sound nice. The doctor had told her that she needed to eat more regularly, and she was trying in every way she knew how to comply with his orders, short of slowing down of course. "Oh, all right. I'll see you at six, then."

Before she could move away from him, he lowered his head and brushed his lips across hers. "I can't wait."

All the way back to the motel her lips tingled, preventing her from calling Sam as she had intended to do from the car. She had to wait until the burning sensation left by Cameron's kisses disappeared. She had to wait a long time.

"You don't want Cabin One again?" George asked, perplexed. "Weren't you comfortable?"

"It was very nice," Melisande said, taking Phyllis's lead and mentally substituting her own definitions for the word *nice*. "It's just that I thought I'd like to try one of your older cabins. You know, see how things were here ten, fifteen years ago."

"Try twenty-five or thirty years ago," George said. "But if that's what you want, then that's what you'll get. Let me fetch my keys and I'll be right back."

They started at Cabin 10 and went toward Cabin 1. In each cabin Melisande tested out the mattress. Only this time she didn't just sit on the bed, she lay down on it. Finally in Cabin 6 she said, "I think this one will do." George heaved a sigh of relief, and she gave him a sympathetic smile, but didn't explain. It was hard for people who didn't suffer from insomnia to understand, but everything had to be just right.

For instance, she reflected a short time later, as she unloaded her car, Cabin 6 had blond furniture that had rounded edges. The carpet was a soft rose color, and though the drapes were faded, they had a pleasing pattern that wasn't too busy. Everything in the cabin worked together to be easy on the eye. Maybe such details didn't matter to the average person, but people who suffered insomnia needed every mental edge they could get.

She opened a window to let some of the perfumed air in, then set about remaking the bed. The mattress was nicely broken in, yet maintained that all-important firmness. It was a hard combination to find. But still she didn't hesitate to spread her egg-crate pad over it. She was convinced that there wasn't a mattress in captivity that couldn't be improved by an egg-crate pad. Except for Aunt Sarah's mattress.

Once she had everything in the room arranged to her liking, she sat cross-legged in the middle of the bed and placed a call to Sam. "How are things?"

"Great. Where are you calling from?"

"I'm still in Lacy."

"No kidding? Then you decided to stay. I think that was the absolutely right decision to make, kiddo. You're long overdue for a rest."

"Don't get so excited," she said grumpily. "I'm not staying to rest. The owner of Aunt Sarah's bed has turned out to be a problem."

"How so?"

Let me count the ways, she thought, raising her eyes to the ceiling. "He can't make up his mind whether he wants to let it go or not, so I said I'd stay over tonight so that we can have dinner and discuss it further."

"Whatever your reason, I'm glad you're staying."

"Why? What's going on there that you don't want me to know about? Have we lost an important account?" She had never left her company for even a day, and she couldn't help but have an uneasy feeling, like a mother who's left her baby unattended. Her company was definitely her baby.

"Relax, Mel. Everything's copacetic."

For the next thirty minutes Sam gave her a rundown on the day's schedule, and they discussed the projects that were in the works, plus the ones they hoped to start within the next couple of weeks.

By the end of their conversation she was feeling a little better. She had even relaxed enough to notice the fragrant scent of the midday breeze that had been filtering into her little cabin. An image of Cameron sprang from the back of her mind to the front. "Sam, do you know of any men's-cologne account we could go after?"

"Not right off the top of my head. Those accounts are usually handled by the big boys up in New York. Why?"

"I've just been thinking about a man's scent, that's all."

"Really?" Sam said with interest. "That's certainly a new occupation for you. Here at home all you ever think about is work."

That was because Cameron wasn't in Dallas. "This *is* work," she said, annoyed, but only with herself. "Who's to say we aren't ready to go after the monster accounts? We may be small, but we have as much talent as any of those agencies in New York."

"Hey, sweetie, calm down. Remember, you're preaching to the converted."

"Right. Well, never mind. I'm sure I'll stop thinking about scent of any kind as soon as I leave this place. Lacy, Alabama, is like one big Disneyland for the senses."

"Whatever you say, Mel," he said in his placating, psychiatrist tone.

"Good-bye, Sam. I'll call you at"—she checked her watch—"four-thirty this afternoon to see how the day has gone. And don't forget to do the things we talked about."

"Yes, Mel. No, Mel. I'll live for your call, Mel."

She hung up and rubbed her forehead. Lord, she was tired. She would love to lie back and take a quick doze, but she never, ever, under any circumstances napped during the day. Napping cut in half her already small chance of sleeping at night.

Wearily she slid off the bed and went to the overnight bag. She scooped out the jean shorts, T-shirt, and underwear, took them into the bathroom and rinsed them out.

She was just draping them over the shower rod when her watch alarm went off. Back in the bedroom, she retrieved two antacid tablets from her purse and downed them. Strangely her stomach hadn't bothered her yet this morning, but the doctor had recommended that she take them every four hours in order to keep her stomach coated.

She looked at her watch, then glanced absently around the cabin. Now what was she going to do?

She was here because a blue-eyed man named Cameron Tate had the only bed in the world she could sleep on. At first sight he had knocked her for a complete loop. And then he had kissed her and kissed her and . . . apparently in the process had warped her brain, because she had agreed to go to dinner with him.

She was out of her natural environment, that was all, and she felt a little lost. It was probably quite natural. But by this time tomorrow she would be on the road back home, and she would be feeling much better.

Four

For the second time that day Melisande hung up from talking to Sam and once again checked her watch. Five-fifteen. That meant Cameron would be here in forty-five minutes. Lord, why had she ever agreed to this dinner?

The bed, she reminded herself. The bed.

She quickly stripped out of her clothes and headed for the shower. It was there, thirty-nine and a half minutes away from the time that Cameron would be picking her up, that it dawned on her she had a wardrobe problem. She was going to have to wear her jeans again, this time with the wrinkled green silk blouse. It wouldn't have been so bad if she had had a decent pair of heels to wear with it, perhaps a nice belt and accent jewelry. But she didn't. All she had was a scruffy pair of tennis shoes.

And the only makeup she had with her was a lipstick, and that was because it was in the purse she had carried to the office the day before she had left Dallas. Noelle wouldn't approve at all. But

who could have predicted she would have felt the
need to dress for success in Lacy, Alabama?

With a moan she leaned forward and gently
banged her head on the shower's tiled wall. She'd
give anything for Noelle to be here, but Noelle was
back in Dallas, exactly where she herself should
be. It was a totally new experience for her to worry
about how she looked, and it was making her a
nervous wreck.

At five twenty-eight Melisande bolted from the
shower. Because she had inadvertently gotten her
hair wet when she was banging her head against
the tile, she quickly applied gel, pulled on her
jeans, wrapped a towel around her and ventured
outside.

After checking to see that no one was about, she
sat on the stoop of the cabin and prayed for the
sun and the breeze to dry her hair quickly. Alter-
nately she monitored her watch and pulled weeds
that were threatening to overgrow the small flower
bed of straggly looking zinnias by the side of the
steps.

By five forty-five she was back in the cabin,
taking antacid tablets. Though it was a while
before her alarm would go off for her next dosage,
she felt she was going to need the extra tablets to
get her through the evening.

It was five fifty-five when Cameron knocked on
the door.

"You're early," she said a bit breathlessly as she
answered the door.

"You're beautiful," he answered.

It wasn't the answer she had expected, and it
took her a minute to recuperate from the impact.
As a rule she shrugged off personal compliments,
but she found she was unable to shrug off his. His
compliment pleased her far more than it should

have. But then, she reacted to him differently than she ever had to anyone else.

He was wearing a pair of dark blue jeans with a sky blue sport shirt, topped by a cocoa-colored sport coat. She should be giving *him* compliments. "Thank you," she said finally.

"You're welcome. Are you ready?"

"Yes." She turned back into the room and grabbed her bag from the bed. "I hope we're going somewhere casual."

"We are. As a matter of fact we're going to one of my favorite places. It's a roadhouse that's tucked away off the main highway. You can get a steak there or you can get a hamburger."

She couldn't resist. "Pecan pie?"

He grinned. "Let's go see."

Several minutes later, she felt compelled to comment, "Your car is very clean." *And big and expensive*, she silently added as she sat in its luxurious depths and enjoyed a virtually bump-free ride as they sped along a back road.

"If I had driven from Dallas to Lacy in the last couple of days, my car would be as dirty as yours."

Heat skittered down her spine. He hadn't even looked at her, yet he had understood her comment. She smoothed her hand over the soft beige leather of the plush, cushioned seat. "What was it that you said you did?"

"Only things that I like."

She nodded, thinking the phrasing of her question had left a great deal to be desired. She had presented him a hole wide enough to drive his car through. If she stayed in Lacy much longer, she would lose all ability to use words effectively.

"I think you should seriously consider being a model. You could make a fortune."

"Really? As much as that?"

The dry tone of his voice told her he wasn't taking her seriously. And, she supposed, if he had the money for a car like this one, he might not be concerned about money. On the other hand, it could be taking everything he had just to make the monthly payments. He remained an enigma, and she deliberately didn't press the issue.

"If I were doing an ad campaign for your car, it would be something like, 'Come fly with me. You can live on board, have meals catered in, and your laundry delivered.'"

He chuckled. "I bet your ad agency is a big success."

"It's not as successful yet as I want it to be, but it's getting there. We're right on the verge of playing in the big leagues."

"You'll get there."

The confidence in his tone warmed her. "Yes, I will. I've worked too hard not to."

He looked at her. Her fingers were idly rubbing the crystal face of her watch, her glorious hair seemed alive with an energy of its own, and her freckles looked adorable, sprinkled across the golden, freshly scrubbed skin of her nose and cheeks. He loved her freckles, he decided, but he hated the circles beneath her eyes. "What did you do today? Did you rest any?"

"Rest?" She repeated the word awkwardly, as if she'd never said it before. "No. I talked with my office a couple of times, and I worked for a while on a new idea." Actually she'd been playing with phrases, trying to come up with an accurate description of the way Cameron smelled. She hadn't been able to do it. "I discussed possible color schemes with George. He's done Cabins 1 and 2 all in beige. I told him I thought he ought to vary it a little. Try blue for instance. Blue is supposed to have a calming effect on people and help them rest better. If it wasn't for my blue bedroom at home, I wouldn't be able to get the few hours of sleep a week I do. Or he could try peach. Women would love it. Peach lights well and makes most any woman look good."

"Is that so?"

"Yes." Noelle often commented on how odd it was that she could be so wonderfully visual with everyone and everything but herself. She couldn't explain it and had never considered the dichotomy of her personality sufficiently important to give it much thought. "I also took a drive around the town. I was amazed at how much I remembered, such as the park, for instance. Aunt Sarah took me there several times. Do they still have concerts there?"

"You bet," he said, wheeling the big car into a sparsely filled parking lot. "As a matter of fact they're just gearing up for their summer season." He switched off the ignition and turned to see her staring through the windshield at the rustic but elegant lodge in front of them. "What do you think of the place?"

"I think I should be dressed better."

"Anything you wear is the right thing to wear, Melisande." He leaned toward her and pressed a light kiss to her cheek, and in another few seconds he was opening the passenger door and extending his hand to her.

Inside, the large dining area was lit for intimacy, and padded leather booths provided both comfort and a degree of privacy. Much to her surprise, there was also a small stage and dance floor.

"This is very nice," she said as she slid into the booth to which they had been shown. She picked up the menu and glanced at it. "Uh-oh. No pecan pie. You're going to be sorry you turned down Mary Ann's dinner."

He smiled. "I don't think so."

Momentarily caught in the charming web of his smile, she stared. "I don't think I've ever known anyone who smiles as much as you do." Or maybe she had, she silently corrected herself, but she had just never known anyone with such a *devastating* smile, a smile that could make her legs and mind go weak at the same time.

"I have a lot to smile about," he murmured.

She buried her head in the menu and studied it with a critical eye. The layout was attractive, with each section clearly lettered. The names of the entrees were written in script, and the description of each entree was written below the name in easy-to-read lettering. "This is a nice job," she murmured.

"What?"

"The menu layout."

"What about the food, Melisande?" he asked, his tone dry. "You're not here for a busman's holiday."

She closed the menu. "Broiled chicken, a baked potato, and a garden salad."

"That's it?"

"And bread. I love bread."

While Cameron gave the waitress their order, Melisande set about rearranging everything on the table, including the cutlery and the glasses. As the waitress walked away, he looked at Melisande and saw what she was doing. He reached across the table and took both of her hands in his.

"Stop," he said. "Okay? Just stop."

Sweet heaven. Even in subdued lighting the intensity of his blue-eyed gaze made her forget time, place, reason. "I'm sorry. Am I making you nervous?"

"No. You're wearing me out."

She grinned. Sam said that sometimes. "I'm sorry," she said again. "I told you, it's hard for me to sit and do nothing."

"Why?"

"I guess it's just that I always have so much to do."

"Tell me what time it is."

She looked at him blankly. "You want to know what time it is?"

"Yes, I do. Tell me precisely what time it is."

The watch he was wearing was gold and looked heavy, masculine, and expensive. She couldn't imagine that it wouldn't have the correct time, but he had asked her for the time. Because his hands still firmly held hers, she had to crane her neck to look at her watch. "It's six twenty-six."

"Okay. It's six twenty-six. So right at this exact moment in time, in this restaurant, in this town, tell me what it is you have to do."

Shore up my defenses against you, because you're definitely dangerous. Knowing it would be wise to keep that reason to herself, she gave him the only other answer she could. "Nothing."

"Then relax, Melisande."

She felt as if her breath were caught in her lungs, and she exhaled a long, shaky breath. "I'll try."

He released her hands and sat back, his eyes on her. "Why is it such an effort for you? What makes you run so hard? Tell me about yourself."

She rolled her shoulders, the subject of herself making her decidedly ill at ease. "You already know everything important. I own an ad agency, and I want Aunt Sarah's bed."

"And that's the sum total of Melisande Lanier? An ad agency and a bed?"

"Those are two very important things. Work and sleep. What else is there?"

"A *personal* life."

A personal life was not a new concept to her. Sam, among others, had preached the necessity of it to her many times. But discussing it with Cameron gave the subject nuances that made her uncomfortable. She took a moment to rearrange the napkin in her lap. "My business *is* my personal life."

"There's no man?"

She shook her head. "A man would get in the way."

"In the way of what?"

Maybe Cameron was a trial attorney or a policeman, she mused. He certainly had the knack of grilling a person. "He would want attention, and if I did give him attention, that would be time I would have to take away from my business. And right now my business needs all my attention."

"But you said it was doing well."

"It is."

"Leave the knife and fork alone, Melisande."

She looked down and saw that she had positioned the utensils so that there was an equal amount of distance between each of them and the plate. It was what she would do if she were supervising a layout that had anything to do with dining, whether it was the place setting, the centerpiece, or the food. She sighed. No matter how instinctive it was for her to rearrange a scene or a display until it was more pleasing to the eye, it wasn't something she normally did when she was having dinner with someone. But being out with Cameron was strangely affecting her nerves. It was with relief that she saw the waitress approach with their salads. "Why don't we talk about you for a while?" she asked after the waitress had left.

"Sure. What would you like to know?"

She started with the subject uppermost in her mind. "Why is Phyllis so determined that you get married?"

His sister's name brought a grin filled with indulgence and love. "Her determination doesn't have to do so much with my getting married as it has to do with distracting herself."

"From what?"

"You heard me ask about her husband?"

She nodded.

"They're going through a rocky spot in their marriage right now, and neither one of them seems to want to face the other with it. And it's a shame. She's as much in love with him as she was ten years ago when she married him, maybe more. And she's completely miserable. I want to help any way I can, even if it's just lending support and an ear."

"You two must be very close."

"In a way we are, I guess. We grew up in a close family."

"You're lucky."

"You didn't?"

Her jaw clenched, and she felt her teeth grind together. "My mother died when I was eight. My father died when I was seventeen. I don't have any brothers or sisters. Why don't we talk about the bed? After all, that's why we're here."

"Did I hear you say *bed*?" a melodic voice asked.

With a silent curse Cameron lifted his head toward the voice, then reluctantly stood. "Elizabeth, what a surprise to see you here."

So this was Elizabeth, Melisande thought. Cameron had called her attractive; he hadn't done her justice. She was beautiful. She had layers of smooth, dark hair and pale, flawless skin. And her elegantly cut royal-blue frock intensified the color of her deep-blue eyes. Maybe it was something in the town's water, Melisande thought sourly, that made all its women have smooth hair and blue eyes.

Elizabeth stared up at Cameron through impossibly thick lashes. "A *pleasant* surprise, I hope."

Deliberately ignoring her comment, he glanced over her shoulder. "Who are you with?"

"My parents. Why don't you come over and say hello to them? They'd love it."

"Maybe some other time. Elizabeth, I'd like you to meet Melisande Lanier. Melisande, this is a friend of my sister's, Elizabeth Cole."

She gazed at the vision of loveliness and forced a smile. "How do you do."

Elizabeth gave a musical laugh. "Fine, I'm sure. And I hope you don't mind if I repeat myself or if I seem overly curious, but I couldn't help but hear you say something about a bed. What on earth are you doing discussing beds, of all things, with Cameron?" Her tone implied the subject was both ludicrous and inappropriate, not to mention a touch perverted.

The beauteous Elizabeth was beginning to grate on Melisande's nerves. Her smile took on a cat-that-licked-the-cream-all-gone expression. "Beds are a favorite subject of mine. I just *love* beds. In fact you could even say I'm *obsessed*, and Cameron's bed in particular holds a special fascination for me."

Elizabeth's pale skin turned a shade paler. "How nice."

Whoa, Melisande thought. Phyllis couldn't hold a candle to the way Elizabeth said the word *nice.*

"I don't believe we've ever met before. Are you a visitor to our town?"

Her smile widened. "Yes."

"A short visit?" Her eyebrows rose with obvious hope.

With a mental groan Melisande took pity on her. She was going to get whiplash if she didn't quit constantly reversing her decision on the woman. "I'm just passing through."

Elizabeth visibly relaxed. "How nice."

At last. *Nice* had been said in a tone that gave the word the correct meaning. But then, Melisande had known her answer would please Elizabeth.

Elizabeth turned back to the main focus of her attention. "Cameron, I hope you enjoyed the meal I brought by yesterday."

"Yes, I did, and as a matter of fact so did Melisande. Thank you for bringing it."

Instantly Elizabeth's attention returned to Melisande. "You ate my food?"

Though she knew there was no need, she couldn't help but feel guilt. "Just a little of it. Mainly the bread. It was really delicious, by the way."

Elizabeth seemed speechless, and Melisande felt a pang of sympathy. But it was only a pang, a very *minuscule* pang.

Cameron began to make motions as if he were getting ready to sit back down. "Thank you for coming over and saying hello, Elizabeth. We don't want to keep you any longer. I'm sure your parents are waiting."

In a way that must have been taught to her in kindergarten class "Southern Princess 101," Elizabeth regained her composure in a flash and fixed her beautiful, wide blue eyes on him. "You're absolutely right, Cameron. I should be getting back to them. How thoughtful of you to think of them. They're such dears, and they think so much of you." She reached lovely, tapered fingers out to his lapel and lightly stroked the material. "There's just one thing. I know how busy you are with the house, but I think you're working entirely too hard, and I simply can't allow it. If you won't look out for yourself, I will." Her smile was brilliant, melting. "I'll be calling you tomorrow with some fun ideas for things for us to do, and I won't take no for an answer, do you hear?"

He shook his head. "I'm sorry, Elizabeth, but my schedule is all filled up."

She placed a coy finger on his lips. "Now what did I tell you? I simply won't listen to a no."

"I'm afraid you're going to have to." His tone was polite, but his expression was decidedly distancing.

She batted her extraordinary lashes at him and laughed liltingly. "We'll just have to see about that, now, won't we?"

"Good-bye, Elizabeth."

"Good-bye for now."

Elizabeth turned away, but she didn't forget her manners and threw a farewell to Melisande over her shoulder. "Good-bye, Millie."

While Cameron and Elizabeth had talked, Melisande had undertaken the rearrangement of her salad into a more picturesque presentation, taking the color and size of the different kinds of lettuce and vegetables into account. But it had been a desultory, indifferent effort and not one of her better jobs. When Cameron returned to his seat across from her, she said, "What's Lisa like?"

"Lisa?" he asked blankly.

"The woman Phyllis prefers for you."

"Why do you want to know?"

"Because I'm thinking of throwing my vote her way."

His mouth twisted ruefully. "At first I thought this little scheme of my sister's was harmless, but it's gotten way out of hand. It's got to stop."

"Are you sure you want it to? I mean, Elizabeth is a beautiful woman. A trifle *obvious*, but beautiful. And I have to admit I'm beginning to have my suspicions that she bakes her bread in one of those new, electric baking machines that produce perfect loaves of bread, no matter how inept you are. However, it does seem as if Phyllis has chosen her candidates well."

His lips quirked. "You think this is all funny, don't you?"

"I have to admit that I do see humor in certain aspects of it," she replied cautiously, then threw caution to the wind. "In fact, in all of it. I'm surprised Phyllis hasn't set up campaign headquarters yet, complete with volunteers and a bank of phones."

"I think she has—in her home."

"Ah." Melisande nodded. "Well, I have to say I can see why the women would be eager to gain your favor. You have a very magnetic quality."

He gazed thoughtfully at her. "You think so?"

Actually she had severely understated the case. "Definitely. Haven't I been saying you should be a model?"

"Forget modeling. Would I be someone you would consider marrying?"

"I—I—" The words stuck in her throat. She tried again. "I don't figure into this, do I? I don't come from Lacy, and I don't have the 'Southern Princess' qualifications Phyllis considers proper. Don't tell her this, but I would actually wear white shoes *after* Labor Day if it wasn't for a friend of mine who cleans out my closet every season."

"Is that a crime?"

"In Lacy it's probably a hanging offense."

"No one would hang you. Your neck is too beautiful."

Instinctively she placed her hand around her throat.

He grinned. "It's not going to happen as Phyllis wants. I'm not going to marry any of her choices, that is, not unless I happen to fall in love with the person."

Her heart grew cold at the idea of him in love with anyone, so cold she couldn't understand why she continued on with the subject. "Perhaps if you gave any of the woman your sister has chosen a chance, you might fall in love with one of them."

He started to say something, and Melisande waited with an anxiousness that vaguely puzzled her. But just then the waitress brought them their dinner. Melisande automatically helped her to arrange the dinner plates and the salad plates so that both could be reached easily.

A silence fell between them while they ate, a silence that at first Melisande wasn't entirely at ease with. She sensed the wheels turning in Cameron's mind, but since she had no idea what he could be thinking, she decided to make an attempt to enjoy the meal.

Cameron's presence across the table disturbed her on a very basic, female level, puzzling her. But as time passed, his presence slowly began to foster contentment in her in an entirely different, equally puzzling way. Maybe it was simply because he seemed happy to be with her rather than with Elizabeth, wherever she was. Was that perverse of her? she wondered. If it was, there seemed to be nothing she could do about it.

By the time the waitress had cleared their dinner away and brought them two cups of decaffeinated coffee, Melisande had relaxed somewhat.

She cleared her throat. "You know, I don't think we've ever seriously discussed money, and I want you to know that I'll pay anything within reason."

He grimaced. "Back to the bed, huh?"

"It's why we're here."

"Okay, Melisande, what do you consider 'reason'?" She named a sum that to him seemed high. "Really?"

"You want more?"

His eyes roved over her. "*Absolutely.*"

The soft huskiness of his voice alerted her, as did the accelerating of her pulse. Thoughts of this morning when she had clung to him, kissing him, and delighting in the feel of his hand on her breast, circled through her mind.

She flushed. "I'm talking about the *bed*, Cameron." Just then the alarm on her watch went off. She punched the button, then reached for her purse and the antacid tablets.

Without comment he watched her take them, then he slowly smiled. "You know what?"

Her expression turned wary. "What?"

"I'm beginning to think you may be right. You *do* need the bed."

Her heart skipped a beat. It was the first thing he had said that had given her any real hope that he might actually sell the bed. "Do you mean that?"

"Yes, I do."

Her mind raced. His comment was definitely a positive sign. Now all she had to do was get him to

name a price. She immediately began to wrestle
with the different approaches she might take.

"The band is really good tonight, don't you
think? Why don't we dance?"

She glanced toward the dance floor and was
surprised to see quite a few couples there, plus
four musicians up on the stage. The place had
filled up since she had last looked. She hadn't
even been aware of the music. She shook her
head. "I can't dance."

"Do you mean you don't know how or do you
mean there's something you think would prevent
you from dancing?"

"A little of both," she admitted reluctantly. "I've
never danced much, plus I've got on tennis shoes.
You can't dance with tennis shoes on."

"You could, or you could take them off. Which is
it to be?"

She frowned as she considered his implacable
expression. "I don't want to dance, Cameron."

"But I do."

She glanced at her watch. No matter how little
sleep she managed to get the night before, adren-
aline kept her going during the day. But this was
the time of night when all the weariness caught up
with her, when she was sure that if she could just
go to bed, she would sleep the sleep of the dead.
The fact that it never happened didn't change the
fact that her body craved rest. "I'd like to go back
to the motel, but I can take a cab if you're not
ready to leave yet."

"Could you sleep if I drove you back now?"

"No."

"We'll leave after a couple of numbers." He held
out his hand to her. "Please. You'll find that
dancing with me is relatively painless."

There were degrees and subtleties of pain, she

thought warily. But there was a warmth in his eyes she couldn't help but respond to. Making the decision to leave on her tennis shoes, she slid from the booth.

The band was playing something slow and dreamily romantic as they walked out on the dance floor. Self-consciously she eyed the well-groomed people who were dancing. In her jeans, tennis shoes, and wrinkled blouse, she felt like a turkey in a room full of peacocks. When Cameron's arm slipped around her waist and pulled her against him, she immediately stiffened.

"Relax," he murmured.

"I am."

His husky chuckle feathered her hair. "Relax," he said again, his voice a deep, soft rumble. "You don't have a thing to do, and you're completely safe."

She could debate how "safe" she was with him, but without being sure why, she let the issue slide. He was easy to follow. His hand at her waist exerted a gentle but firm guidance, and they fit disconcertingly well together, just as they had on the bed this morning. As if her body held a memory of him and that time, her breasts pressed against his broad chest and her pelvis nestled intimately into his. Slowly her surroundings receded as the feel of him began to dominate her thoughts, and she forgot about her impatience to leave.

Tonight there was a sexual spiciness to his scent, a blatant maleness. He radiated strength and a tangible sexuality she couldn't deny. If she hadn't been so tired, she might have felt the need to stay on the alert. If she hadn't had the strange sense that he was keeping a tight rein on that very basic, fundamental passion that was so much a part of him, she might have grown alarmed. As it was, she allowed herself to lower her barriers and trust for this short space of time.

She sank against him, closed her eyes, and gave herself up to the seductive rhythm of their bodies moving together. There was no nagging pain in her stomach, no ad campaigns in her mind. She shut her brain down and discovered contentment. She swayed with him and let the music wrap soothingly around her.

Sometime later she found herself sitting beside Cameron, surrounded by the soft luxury of the big car as it purred down the road, and she closed her eyes, just to rest them until she got to the motel.

Five

Melisande heard a vaguely familiar sound, and she had to fight her way up through heavy layers of sleep before she realized it was her watch alarm going off. Automatically her hand shot toward the bedside table and her watch there.

Her hand encountered covers.

Without opening her eyes, without rolling over, she managed to shift slightly to the left and again reached her hand toward the table.

She encountered more covers.

She must have gotten turned around in the bed, she thought drowsily, and tried to orient herself. The still-beeping alarm sounded close by. She patted the area of the bed near her where she judged the sound was coming from. But what was her watch doing in the bed, anyway? She always took it off and placed it on the left-hand night-stand.

She felt a slight pressure on her wrist, and the annoying alarm ceased. Before she had time to work through what had happened, the mattress sagged and a hand pushed her hair away from her eyes. "Are you ready to wake up or do you want to go back to sleep?"

At the sound of Cameron's soft, husky voice, her eyes flew open. He was sitting on the side of the bed, staring down at her. She must have forgotten to take off her watch last night, and the pressure she had felt on her wrist had been him turning off the alarm. But that left one very important question unanswered.

"What are you doing here?"

"I live here."

"In my motel room?"

"No. In my house."

His house? She levered herself upright and twisted around until she was sitting up. Shoving a mass of curls away from her face, she glanced around her. The French doors stood partially open, allowing sunlight to cascade across the bare-wood floor and the dark needlepoint rug. The long, gracefully arching mirror hung above the three chests. The faint scent of roses, coffee, and Cameron hung in the air.

Lord, he was right! She was in his house. And that wasn't all. She was also in his *bed.*

She waited until the reverberations of the thunderous shock died. Then she quietly asked, "What am I doing here?"

"You fell asleep in the car last night on the way home, and I decided I should bring you here."

"Why?"

"I didn't know what you'd done with your motel key, I didn't want to go through your purse, I didn't want to chance waking up George to ask him for an extra key, and I sure as hell didn't want to wake you up once you'd gotten to sleep." He shrugged. "Take your pick of reasons."

She might still have been asleep for all the

meaning she got from his explanation. In contrast to how she knew she appeared, he looked fresh and vital in a pair of clean blue jeans and a beige and blue patterned shirt that was pulled together at the edges, but not buttoned. Every now and then she caught a glimpse of dark curly chest hair. She tore her gaze away from his chest and fixed him with the steadiest gaze she could manage at the moment. "Explain that to me again, but this time explain it to me another way so that I'll understand."

"When you fell asleep in the car, I didn't want to wake you up, so I took a chance and brought you here." He forestalled her next why, by adding, "And it worked. You slept all night."

Her expression turned stunned. "I slept—you're *right*. I slept the *entire* night." A smile of genuine delight spread across her face.

And watching the smile, Cameron felt something shift in his heart, something big, important, and basic. "How do you feel?"

The smile faded as she made a cautious assessment. "Rested. Not tired. I—Wait a minute." She looked down at herself and grabbed the tail of her green silk blouse that had come loose from her jeans. "I'm still dressed."

His lips twitched. "Much as I regret it, yes, you are. I took off only your shoes. Believe me, I would have loved to take off much more, but I didn't think you'd like it." He watched the varied emotions flash across her face. "Was I wrong?"

"No, of course you weren't wrong." Hearing her sharp tone, she plowed her fingers through her tangled hair and re-formed her reply. "Thank you."

"For what?" he asked, amused. "For not taking advantage of you? No thanks are necessary. I was being selfish. When you and I make love, Melisande, I want you fully conscious and as crazed for me as I am for you."

An insidious heat crawled through her, took possession of everything vital in her, and wouldn't let go. "You know, Cameron," she said steadily, "there are a great many things wrong with what you just said, and I'll start with the word *when*. You said *when* we make love, as if the act of our lovemaking was a fact. Trust me, it's not. We are *not* going to make love, Cameron—awake, asleep, or any other way."

Something flickered in the depths of his blue eyes, but his tone was mild. "Fine. If that's the way you want it."

"It is."

"But don't fault me if I try to change your mind."

His scent seemed to be all around her, that sensual, masculine, tantalizing scent that had the ability to bend a woman's brain waves. She would have thought a good night's sleep would have strengthened her resolve against him. In fact it seemed to have done the opposite. Her senses were alarmingly alert, making her all the more aware of him. "Is that coffee I smell?" she asked, her voice barely above a whisper.

He picked up a steaming mug from a side table and handed it to her. She took it, but gazed at it uncertainly. "Did you bring this up for me?"

He shook his head. "I wasn't sure when you'd wake up. If I had known you had that damned alarm set, I would have turned it off so that you could have slept longer."

"But the coffee." She gestured to the mug with her free hand.

"I had originally poured it for me, then carried it

up with me when I came to check on you. But go ahead. I've already had several cups."

She didn't need another invitation. She sipped at the coffee, fervently wishing it had caffeine in it. She felt as if she needed a good jolt to restore her common sense. "I must have really slept hard. I remember us dancing, and I remember being in the car, and then that's it." Her eyes widened. "It's actually kind of frightening to me. Nothing like that has ever happened before. I always know exactly where I am and what I'm doing."

His voice was reassuring as his fingers idly played with a tightly coiled ginger curl. "There's nothing to be frightened of. You obviously needed the sleep badly, and you were finally able to get it."

"Yes . . ." Something was nagging at the back of her mind, something important. "You said you've already had several cups of coffee?"

"I've been up a while."

"Do you normally get up so early?"

He folded his arms across his chest. "Not usually, but then I didn't sleep well last night."

There was something not quite right, she thought, scanning the bed. The crocheted coverlet had been neatly folded down to the foot, but the rest of the covers and pillows were tossed and tangled, almost as if the whole bed had been used in the night. How odd. As deeply as she had slept, she would be surprised if she had moved an inch. "Cameron," she said, taking care to pronounce her words slowly and clearly, "where did you sleep last night?"

His blue-eyed gaze never wavered from her face. "Where I sleep every night. In my bed."

"In your—" Her fingers twitched. Coffee sloshed over the cup's rim and onto the back of her hand. She placed the cup on the side table nearest her, admonishing herself to remain as calm as possible. It did no good. "You mean you and I *slept* together?"

"Yes. And, Melisande"—his hand reached out to her, and long fingers angled up the side of her face, gently holding her head still, ensuring that her gaze remained on him—"as hard as it was on me, that's *all* we did. Sleep."

"But why in the world didn't you sleep someplace else?" She was hard put not to sputter.

He dropped his hand back to his side. "Why should I? This is the bed I sleep in. I told you that right from the start."

"Then why didn't you put me in another bed?"

"Mainly because this is the bed you've been wanting to sleep in ever since you arrived."

"No, Cameron. I've been trying to *buy* the bed, not sleep in it."

"Same difference."

She slid off the bed to her feet, badly needing to feel something solid beneath her. But the floor didn't provide the secure feeling she so urgently needed. She paced to the French doors, but quickly returned to stand in front of him. "You know, you make it sound as if you made the only logical, possible choice, but that's just not the case. We never in a million years should have slept together."

"Why not? Nothing happened."

"Cameron, we're not children at a slumber party. We're adults, a man and a woman who . . . who . . ."

"Who are strongly attracted to each other," he finished for her, his voice low and somewhat rough. "Yes, Melisande, I know. Believe me, I'm very much aware of my attraction to you. Actually *attraction* is too mild a word for the way I feel about you. *On fire for you* would be more accurate."

"Please don't say things like that."

He levered himself off the bed to his feet. "Why not? It's true. Like you said, we're both adults, and I've tried to be very up-front with you. I want you, and I think you want me too. And that knowledge, Melisande, is why it was damned near impossible for me to get much sleep last night. I kept wanting to put my arm around you and draw you to me, but I knew if I gave in to the urge, I wouldn't be able to stop."

It would be worth losing sleep and much more to make love to Cameron. The thought came unbidden and shook her down to her toes. "Nothing can happen between us."

"You're going to have to do a powerful job of convincing me of that, because I can't think of a reason in the world why it can't."

"Because."

"Because? Try again, Melisande."

The morning light made his eyes seem all the more discerning, and once again she received the impression he could see straight through her. More than that, he could see things in her that she couldn't. She turned away from him. "I've already told you, I can't stay here. My life is back in Dallas."

He circled her until he was standing in front of her. "That wouldn't stop you from coming here during vacations and for holidays."

She shook her head. "I don't take vacations or holidays."

"Big mistake, Melisande. Big mistake."

"The way I choose to live my life is none of your business."

His hands came down on her shoulders, and he

brushed the pads of his thumbs up and down the side of her throat. "You know, you're very sexy in the morning with your hair in this unrestrained tangle. But then, you're sexy anytime."

Excitement coiled through her and mingled with heat. She couldn't recall anyone ever calling her sexy. It made her feel womanly and dangerously close to losing her inhibitions. "I need to . . . uh . . ." Her tongue flicked out to moisten her dry lips while she tried to order her thoughts.

She looked so soft, so utterly vulnerable, so desirable. How could a woman make him feel as if he wanted to throw her on her back and cover her body with his, he wondered, and at the same time make him feel as if he would move heaven and earth to protect her—if necessary, even from himself? His arousal pressed uncomfortably against his jeans, and though he knew he was going to pay a high price for his gallantry, he nevertheless let her off the hook. "I was about to start breakfast. Why don't you wash up? In fact take a bath if you like. Help yourself to anything in the bathroom you need. By the time you're finished, I should have breakfast on the table. We'll eat out on the porch again. It's a great morning." Not able to trust himself with her for even one more minute, he walked quickly from the room.

Melisande exhaled slowly, trying to analyze what was happening to her. Because of the full night's sleep she had had, she felt physically better than she had in a long time, but a major disturbance lingered in her bloodstream.

What if something *had* happened between them? she asked herself. What if . . . ?

The answer was simple. If she had just spent a night in Cameron's arms, she would now be feeling a pleasure-sated satisfaction that would go clear through her bones. And it would have been a night she would remember for the rest of her life.

She stood utterly still as she reflected on the answer she had just given herself. But she wasn't courageous enough to contemplate for long the enormity of her answer or its ramifications. She hurried into the next room.

The bathroom was large and had all of its original fixtures. One immense white-and-blue colored leaded-glass window admitted softly filtered light. The tub was the same oversized, four-footed, free-standing one that Melisande had used on her long-ago visit, but the curtain around it and the shower head above it had been installed since then.

She turned her attention to the glass shelves that held Cameron's toiletries suspended above the pedestal basin. Running her fingers along the edge of the shelves, she carefully studied the things he used as if they might give her clues about him, his makeup, his chemistry, and why he seemed to have such an effect on her. It would have been nice to discover the brand of cologne he wore, she thought, but she didn't find one bottle. It backed up her theory that his scent was unique to him.

She showered, using his shampoo and soap. But even though both were unscented, she couldn't get Cameron's scent from her nostrils or his image from her mind. This morning she didn't need the tingling spray of the shower to wake her up. The world was already in sharp, shining focus, and Cameron was her world's focal point.

She needed to get out of Lacy, Alabama, in the worst way, she concluded. Something had happened to her since she had been here, something she couldn't explain. But she had the feeling that if she allowed herself to relax even a little, she might lose something vitally important to her.

The feeling caused her no astonishment. If Cameron could interfere with something as fundamental as her breathing pattern, he could certainly interfere with her life.

After toweling off, she again dressed in her jeans and the now badly wrinkled green silk blouse. Then she lightly combed her fingers through her wet hair and said a quick "hair prayer" that it wouldn't dry before she had a chance to get back to the motel and subdue it with gel.

The floorboards creaked as she walked down the wide hallway, her pace slowing when she neared the stairs. As a child she had explored every nook and cranny of the house. Both inside and out, Aunt Sarah's home had been a wonderland of eccentricity and fantasy. It had given her peace when she had badly needed it, and the chance to be a child without worries for a short, but important period of time. And now she was about to leave. But not just yet, she decided, not without exploring one last time.

Minutes later, as she wandered from room to room, she realized that there had been some amazing changes. Extensive work had been done on all the rooms, and the furniture, except for in the big bedroom where she had just spent the night, had been removed.

There hadn't been another bed he could have slept in.

The last room she entered was at the back side of the house and overlooked the gardens and the river. This room would make a great nursery, she thought absently. Even without furniture and bare walls it seemed a peaceful, happy room. A mother could nurse her baby in a rocking chair by the windows or lie on a quilt on the floor and play with her child. . . .

"I attacked the structural problems first," Cameron said, his voice low.

Feeling unaccountably guilty at getting caught in the middle of such an outlandish, impractical daydream, she wheeled to find him standing in the doorway. He had buttoned his shirt, she noticed with an emotion that wavered precariously between gratitude and disappointment. "Like what?"

He had chosen the neutral subject of the house quite deliberately. After their earlier heated confrontation, he hoped it would put her at ease. The problem was, *he* didn't feel at ease. Talking was the last thing he wanted to do with her.

He slipped his hands into his pockets and strolled into the room. "I'm adding bathrooms and closets to every upstairs bedroom, plus additional closets and bathrooms downstairs. It was a tricky situation to convert existing space into what I wanted without destroying the integrity of the remaining space. Fortunately the rooms are large enough that I was able to do it without losing too many of the details that I find so charming about the house."

Maybe he was an architect. In spite of herself she was becoming more and more curious about what he did for a living. "Have you done this kind of thing before?"

"No, but I've had a lot of fun learning. Have you been through all the rooms up here?" At her nod he asked, "What do you think?"

"It looks as if you've done a great job so far. If I didn't already know better, I might not have known those bathrooms and closets had recently been added. Everything looks as if it belongs."

"Thank you." A tension that had nothing to do

with sexual need eased from him. "I'm glad you approve, particularly since you have good memories of the place. It means a lot."

The warmth of his tone seared her nerves. "You certainly don't need my approval," she snapped, instinctively reaching for contrariness in hopes that it would shield her. Unfortunately she knew it would take far more than an attitude to protect her.

His gaze sharpened. "I didn't say I did. I simply said I was glad."

She made a nonchalant gesture, hoping to give the impression she didn't care one way or the other. "By the way, where is the furniture?"

"In temporary storage. I didn't want to take the chance that any of it might get damaged while the work was going on. I'll eventually be redoing the bedroom I'm using, but I had to keep a few rooms I could live in."

She decided to drop her uncaring pretense; it wasn't working anyway. "You know, even without seeing the furniture it's easy to visualize what should go where and even how the walls and windows should be decorated. Anyone who comes here to stay for whatever reason will be very comfortable and have a great time in the bargain."

"Would you?"

Her fingers automatically went to her watch, but she didn't look at it. "Sure. If I had the time. The problem is I don't."

"You're repeating yourself, Melisande."

"Maybe I think if I say it often enough, you'll believe me."

"Then you can quit saying it, because I believe you."

She turned away, hurt and disappointed without knowing why. Forcing her thoughts to her surroundings, she tried to see in her mind's eye what it would look like when he was finished. "What else are you doing to the house?"

"Downstairs we had to tear into some walls and replace the plumbing. I've also pulled down a lot of modern paneling to get to the original wall, and in some rooms we've uncovered fireplaces that had been paneled or walled over."

Her eyes widened. "Why would Aunt Sarah do that?"

He shrugged. "You forget how many years she lived here. Styles change, and women like to decorate. Through the years she probably went through several style changes. I've found eight and ten coats of paint covering the most beautiful wood." He moved to the window and looked out. "I'm just taking my time, making sure things are done right."

As if he had beckoned her, she followed him to the window. "It would almost be worth a trip back here just to see what the house looks like when you get through with it. I bet it's going to be beautiful."

"I can guarantee that it will be."

Maybe one day she would drive through Lacy, she thought, and stop by the house, just to see what he had done. But she wouldn't get out and walk up to the door. She wouldn't ring the bell and wait to see what woman came to the door, what woman he had chosen. "What do you have planned for the gardens? Those roses down there are going to be choked out if you don't do something soon."

"I've already hired a landscaper. He'll be here in a couple of days with a crew of workers."

Her head jerked around to him. "A landscaper? Are you making changes in the gardens too?"

His shoulders lifted and fell. "I have no dramatic changes in mind. I'll see what he recommends."

He regarded her thoughtfully as she stared down at the garden, her bottom lip caught between her teeth. "Why? Is there something you'd like to see done?"

She didn't know the first thing about gardening, but amazingly she did have a few ideas that centered around the core of what remained of Aunt Sarah's gardens, a sense of colors and patterns that she felt would be absolutely right. Her ideas didn't matter though, she reminded herself, because neither the gardens nor the house were any of her concern. "No, I was simply curious." For the first time since she had awakened, she looked at her watch, and was surprised to see that it was already eight-thirty. "Is breakfast ready? I have a lot to do before I leave, and you and I still have a deal to make."

He rocked back on his heels. "That's right. You're leaving today. In that case we'd better go on down. As it happens, breakfast is on the table, waiting for us. That's what I came up to tell you. I hope you're hungry."

"I am," she said, preceding him out the door and down the stairs. "You know, it's funny, but I don't normally eat as much or as often as I have since I've been here."

"Then you must starve in Dallas, because you haven't eaten that much, at least not when we've been together."

"I don't starve. I just eat on the run."

"Which means you're eating too fast and not enough of what's good for you."

"Jeez, Cameron, you sound just like my doctor."

His hand shot out, stopping her. "Your doctor? Have you been sick?"

The seriousness in his expression surprised her. "No. It's just the insomnia and the occasional stomach pang. Nothing I can't handle." Ignoring his clearly dubious expression, she crossed the entry hall to the front door and stepped outside.

The air was fresh and warm, and the roses looked almost pearlized. Sunlight created a spectrum of shades in the Spanish moss that ranged from gray to green, and the scented breeze coaxed them into a graceful dance.

She drew a deep breath. "What a beautiful morning. The chamber of commerce should take a picture of this day and put it in a brochure. Tourists would come by the thousands."

Having followed her out, he chuckled. "Lacy wouldn't know what to do with thousands of tourists. And anyway Lacy's chamber of commerce is more of a social organization than a serious business to promote the town."

Moving down the porch, she gave some thought to what he'd said. "I suppose that's best. After all, Lacy wouldn't be Lacy with tourists overrunning the place."

Just then she noticed the table. A low arrangement of roses graced its center, their pink and yellow colors complemented by a crystal pitcher of orange juice, a small bowl of plum preserves, and another containing a stick of golden butter. And at each place setting there was a bowl of fresh strawberries and a crisply folded aqua cloth napkin. "When did you do all this? The table is lovely."

"I told you, I've been up for a while, and thanks for the compliment. But if the table turned out attractive, it was an accident, I can assure you.

"I'm not sure I believe that. From what little I've seen, you're pretty good at whatever you try." It was another perfect opportunity to find out what he did for a living, but she rushed on. "And this"—she gestured at the table—"would make a terrific orange-juice shoot."

"I beg your pardon?" he said, seating her, then dropping into the chair across from her.

She laughed. "I'm sorry. I tend to think in terms of how best to sell a product. It's a habit."

He didn't think he had ever heard her laugh before. It was a sweet, clear, infectious sound that made him want to pull her into his arms and kiss her breathless. The hand on his knee clenched and unclenched. All in good time, he told himself. All in good time. "Well, forget selling for just a little while longer and eat." He held a basket of hot biscuits toward her. "Have one."

She eyed them suspiciously. "Which prospective bride baked these?"

"*I* baked them."

"*You?*"

His lips quirked. "Don't get too excited. They came from a pop-open can."

With a smile she took two. "I'll bet they're delicious." And they were, as was the rest of the breakfast. And while the meal wasn't exactly nerve-free, it was pleasant. She and Cameron were quiet while they ate, and when one of them did speak, it was to make an idle comment or to request that an item on the table be passed. The domesticity of the scene had her wanting to run and, in the next minute, wanting to stay forever.

It was wonderful, *too* wonderful. Normally she didn't, couldn't, enjoy anything that progressed at a leisurely pace, but inexplicably she found herself eating slowly.

She put down her fork and worriedly fingered her watch. Days before, the idea of a gentle, peaceful morning, complete with swaying Spanish moss, perfumed air, and a mesmerizing man would never have appealed to her. But here she was, smack in the middle of a genuine Kodak moment.

And if someone snapped their picture, it could be used in women's magazines all across the nation. The caption would read:

Domestic bliss, yours for the asking.

Except, because of the business she was in, she knew better than most that appearances were deceiving. She had just spent a night in his bed, a platonic night, a totally *unconscious* night, in which absolutely *nothing* had happened. The fact rankled, and because it did, the state of her nerves began to degenerate.

She changed her mind about how she would use their picture. If she were to use this scene in an advertisement, she would have the caption below it read:

Beware. Atmosphere may induce severe brain damage.

She pushed her plate to the side, placed her elbows on the table, and leveled a serious gaze on Cameron.

"Okay, this is it. The time is here for you to make your decision. Last night at the roadhouse you said you thought I might be right after all. That I did need the bed. And if nothing else, my staying here last night proved it. That was the first full night's sleep I've had in at least a year. If I had any doubts, my theory about Aunt Sarah's bed—excuse me, *your* bed—has been proven. I can't sleep in any other bed but that one."

"How do you know?"

"I know because I've probably tried out every kind of mattress there is. And you wouldn't believe how many kinds there are or their stupid names. They start with Comfortable and go right to Extra Comfortable, Super Comfortable, Luxury Ultra Comfortable, Ultra Plush Comfortable, and the list goes on and on. But the names mean nothing. You have to try them out."

"Which you have."

"I've not only tried them out in the store, I must have bought at least a dozen. And no matter how expensive or customized the mattress, it always felt to me as if there was a huge boulder lodged beneath it. Even on a good night I've never been able to get more than two hours of solid sleep on any of them. Eleven of them went back to the store after one night. The only reason I have the twelfth is that I gave up."

"Until you thought of the bed upstairs."

"That's right. It can't be duplicated. Believe me, if I thought it could, I would try. But"—she shook her head—"the bed and mattress are a combination not only of craftsmanship but also of over eighty years of wear by Sarah and her family. To get another mattress to feel exactly like that would be impossible. It's one of a kind." She sat back and gazed at him. "There. If you didn't know before, you now know you have an extremely valuable commodity to sell. At least to one buyer. So name your price."

Just looking at her made him want to smile. The shadows were still beneath her eyes, but they had faded considerably. And her eyes were sparkling with a new vitality. He was helping her, and while he was at it, he was falling in love with her. Hard. There was no way out of it for him. No way of explaining it. In retrospect he could see that she had walked into his heart as easily as she had walked into his house. But however it had happened, he had no intention of letting her leave now.

He managed a worried expression. "I'm sorry, Melisande. I really am. But I have the same dilemma I had yesterday. I have to consider the value of the bed as it relates to the house. And before I can fully come up with that value, I have to decide what I'm going to do with the house." He exhaled heavily. "I have a lot of decisions to make."

Yesterday she had been patient. Today she wanted to throw something. Resisting the urge, she clasped her hands tightly together. "And just how long do you think it's going to take you to make all these decisions?"

"I'm not sure. As I said, I have a *lot* of decisions to make."

She opened her mouth, intending to make a biting comment, but he held up his hand, forestalling her.

"Don't worry. I plan to get help with some of them."

Her forehead knitted. "*Help?* What kind of help?"

"I'm going to hire an interior decorator to help me decide on wall and window treatments. Or are they called interior designers these days?"

It seemed to her as if, subject-wise, they had just taken a drastic left turn, but as it happened, she had firm opinions on decorators. "Whatever they're called, I think hiring one is an extremely bad idea."

"Why?"

"Because you're going to end up with a house that *looks* decorated. You'll be living in something that feels like a hotel or a museum instead of a home. I know, because I live in a house like that, but it's all right for me because I'm rarely home. I wouldn't even have bothered with a decorator except that the person who coordinates my clothes decided my house needed to be coordinated too."

"Someone coordinates your clothes?"

"You don't think I dress like this all the time, do you?"

"What's wrong with the way you're dressed? I think you look great."

With very little effort a woman could grow to prize a man like him. *If* she let herself. "The point, Cameron, is that you run the danger of getting someone who wouldn't understand this house, how wonderful it is, how special. And besides that, an interior designer would cost you a fortune."

"I guess I hadn't thought about the matter in that light."

"Well, think about it. You'd be much better off doing it yourself."

He shook his head, making a valiant effort to keep a straight face. "There's no telling what I'd get if I did it myself."

"Nonsense," she said, frowning, wondering how she had let the subject of the bed get so far away from her. "I would think choosing wallpaper, fabric, and paints would be fairly simple. All you have to do is keep the character of the house in mind and back that knowledge up with your own taste."

He could manage a blank look for only a few seconds, after which his expression returned to normal, reflecting his natural intelligence. "I'll tell you what, Melisande. I'll make you a deal."

"Deal?" she asked, suddenly aware that she might have just been had.

"Stay here for a week and—"

"A *week*! Are you out of your mind? There's no way I can do that."

"You haven't heard my deal yet."

"I heard the first part of it, and it's impossible."

"The last part concerns the bed."

Dammit. "The bed?"

"The bed."

She sighed. "All right. Let's hear the rest."

"As I was saying, stay here for a week. Help me make the decisions about the garden and the house, go with me to the Founders Day Dance—"

She rose half out of the chair. "*Dance?* Why would I want to go to a dance? No way! That's just not possible. You're going to have to think of something else." She had danced with him last night for a very short time and ended up sleeping in his bed. There was no telling where an entire night of dancing might lead.

He looked at her, his eyebrows arched, his blue eyes laser sharp. "Apparently, since you keep interrupting, you don't want to hear the last part of the deal—the part that concerns the *bed*."

She sank back into the chair. "Has anyone ever told you that you're completely unscrupulous?"

"Many times. Now are you going to listen?" At her reluctant nod, he went on. "Attend the dance as my date, and at the end of the week I promise you I will have made a decision about what to do with the house and whether or not I want to sell the bed."

"What kind of deal is that?" she asked, incensed. "You get everything, and I get nothing." That wasn't entirely true. She would get to spend a whole week with him. Instinct told her it might prove to be the most memorable week of her life;

her heart told her it might not be able to take the strain.

"What you get, Melisande, is the chance that I will sell you the bed. If you leave today, there will be *no* chance that I will sell you the bed."

She was going to throw something. She was most definitely going to throw something. The only question was what. She scanned the table and spotted the bowl of plum preserves. She drew it to her and allowed her fingers to stroke its edge. In some curious, metaphysical way, the feel of the stoneware bowl beneath her fingertips soothed her.

"I have some questions."

He gestured with his hands. "Fire away."

"Why did you include the Founders Day Dance in the deal?"

"It'll get my sister off my back, at least on that particular subject. Otherwise, she's going to nag me to death until I agree to take one of her friends."

It was a good reason, she thought as an image of Elizabeth flashed into her mind. It might have been nice, in a purely impersonal way, to have him say that he actually wanted the pleasure of going with her, but knowing he had asked her only because he wanted to avoid taking a real date was far better. The knowledge would help her keep their arrangement on a business level in her mind. *If* she agreed.

"What about asking your sister to help you with the house?"

"I don't want to give Phyllis an excuse to spend more time than she already has away from what she should be concentrating on, namely her marriage."

Another good reason. "What about asking one

of her friends to help you with the house? I'm sure they have exquisite taste. Well, maybe not Elizabeth, but the others—"

"I'm afraid my intentions would be misread, that whoever I asked to help me might presume that she would one day soon be mistress of the house she was decorating. I know you wouldn't think that. In a week you'll be gone. Right? And you've already made it clear to me that it won't work between us. So there would be no misunderstanding."

Her hand gripped the bowl of preserves. "You are asking the impossible of me."

"Then you *do* think it might work out between us?"

She hit the side of the bowl of preserves with the flat of her hand. It went flying across the smooth glass tabletop and right off the edge.

Cameron caught it a second before it would have landed in his lap and calmly replaced it on the table. "Consider it a business deal, Melisande. At the end of which, instead of winning an account, you'll win the bed."

"Will I, Cameron?"

He spread his hands wide. "Like any business venture, there's a risk. But sometimes risks can bring great rewards."

She jerked up from the table and walked to the porch railing. What had started out so simple in her mind—a two-day trip to fetch the bed—had turned out to be intricately complicated. She leaned back against the railing. "Look, the bed is very important to me, but . . ." Why was she hesitating? She couldn't stay here another day, much less another week. And she needed to tell him just that.

He rose, went to her, and took her hand. "I know

you'd be doing it for the bed, but you'd also be doing me a great favor."

The blue depths of his eyes glimmered hypnotically, and she forgot what it was she needed to tell him. "You confuse me, Cameron. You really do."

He brought her hand to his mouth. His lips nuzzled the sensitive skin of her palm, then he lightly trailed the tip of his tongue across it. "There's nothing to be confused about," he murmured, his mouth against her palm.

Heat crawled into her veins, and desperation tinged her tone. "There's everything in the world to be confused about. It wasn't all that long ago that you were talking about making love with me, and now you're presenting me with a business deal."

He stiffened. "Listen to me, Melisande. Making love to you is something I want to happen so much, I'm nearly crazy with it. But my need for you will stay separate from my final decision on the bed. Selling you the bed is not contingent on you sleeping with me, and don't for a minute think it is. The last thing I want or intend is for you to feel pressured into my arms." His voice dropped lower, and he edged closer to her. "I told you before and I'll tell you again. Whether or not we make love is going to be up to you, but you should know, my body is not going to know any peace until I'm buried deep inside you, and when I am, we're both going to enjoy the hell out of it. I guarantee it."

She drew a quick breath, overwhelmed by him, by his words, by the fire in his eyes, and by the fire in her lower body. She was out of her element and dangerously close to being out of her mind. Because at that moment she wanted nothing more than to wrap her arms around his neck and pull him to her.

She never had a chance to find out if she would have followed through with the urge, because he took a step back from her. Still holding her hand, he used his other hand to tenderly caress an overly energetic ginger curl. "Let me take you into the front parlor and show you the wallpaper and paint-chip samples I have. It will give you a better idea of what I'm talking about."

She nodded, because right at that moment she would have agreed to anything he asked of her.

Six

As soon as Melisande walked into the front parlor, she was immediately struck by a feeling of familiarity. Considering it had been many years since she had been in the room, there was no rhyme or reason to her feeling, and she finally decided simply to chalk it up to the heightened state of her senses.

Unfortunately distance between her and Cameron wasn't helping with that particular problem. He stood at a long worktable that consisted of two sheets of plywood placed over four sawhorses, and was sorting through a stack of file folders. His concentration belied the fact that he had just uttered the most outrageous, blood-heating, knee-weakening words to her that anyone had ever uttered to her.

But since his attention was elsewhere, it gave her the opportunity to regain her equilibrium and become reacquainted with the room. It was the largest in the house, with windows that looked out onto the porch, the roses, and the lawn beyond. Three panes were stained glass and set into a bay window, the middle being a Tiffany-like wisteria pattern, the two side ones done in light-catching white and gold.

Even without most of its furniture and despite the presence of the worktable, the room was sunny, airy, and completely charming.

Cameron found the folder for which he had been searching, and straightened away from the worktable. "As you can see, I think I must have every wallpaper-sample book and paint-chip folder there is."

"You do seem to have explored the market." Wallpaper sample books were stacked waist high against two walls, and boxes that contained color samples and upholstery material took up another entire wall. "Why so many?"

"Because I don't know what I want. I've never done anything like this before, not to a house, at any rate."

"You've decorated something else?" She tried to imagine what it might have been.

"Let's just say I had a visual concept of what I wanted for another project, but for this house, the only concept and criterion I have is comfort. I want it to be a place in which people can relax."

"Well, I agree with you there, and I don't think it will be hard to achieve. But Cameron, I'm still not sure I'm the one to help you."

"Why not?"

"For several reasons." She deliberately chose to omit her fear that she would become too distracted by him to be able even to pick out something as simple as a color of paint. "Besides the fact that I have no experience in doing anything like this, I don't remember the furniture. And to do a proper job, the contents of each room would need to be taken into account. You said you didn't acquire all the furniture, but what you did get would need to be coordinated with any new pieces you decided you needed. Everything has to work together as a whole, the wood, the upholstery fabric, the wallpaper, the paint, and the draperies—at least that's what I've been told. And then there's any pictures or paintings you might have." She shook her head. "This would be an enormous job and would take much longer than a week."

"I'm not asking you to do every room, top to bottom. Just start with the main rooms and see how much you can accomplish."

She threw up a hand. "The last time I saw the furnishings, Cameron, I was eight years old. When you're that age, you don't spend your time checking out how a house is decorated. Except for one or two pieces, I have only vague impressions of the furniture." She shook her head. "It would be impossible."

"I'm surprised at you, Melisande. I wouldn't have thought *impossible* was a word in your vocabulary."

His eyes were twinkling again, and her defenses were cracking. "I don't normally, but—"

He cut her off by handing her the folder he had been holding. "This should help."

"What's this?"

"Before I put everything into storage, I took a complete inventory of each room, along with color photos of each piece of furniture, showing its location and position in regard to the other furniture in the room."

She barely resisted the urge to make a face. "How very thorough of you."

He smiled slowly, charmingly. "I know how to go about getting what I want, Melisande. I always have."

She didn't doubt him for a second. He radiated magnetism, self-confidence, and a power all the more forceful because it was so understated.

"So are you going to give me what I want?"

A vision flashed into her mind of the two of them tangled together in bed, their naked bodies covered with sweat, their bodies moving urgently together. He wanted it, and Lord help her, she wanted it.

"Will you stay . . . and help me with the house?"

She tried to swallow and found she couldn't. "What?"

He ambled to her, closing the distance between them, until he was near enough that she could have sworn she could hear his heart beating. It sounded loud in her ears, a heart beating with strong, raw desire. And then she realized it was her heart she was hearing, her desire that was threatening to strangle her.

"Say you'll stay," he said huskily. "I need you to stay. I need you."

The worst had happened. She had lost not only the ability to use words, but also the ability to understand words being spoken to her. "You need me? For the house . . . or for you?"

He slid his hand beneath her hair and around the back of her neck and bent his head to her. "Don't you know? Can't you feel it? I need you more with every breath I take, but since I've left what's going to happen between us up to you, I'll have to settle for the house." His eyes dropped to her lips. "Unless you've made up your mind about us? In which case I'll call the workmen, tell them to take the day off, and we'll go upstairs. In five minutes I'll be so deep inside you, you'll never be able to get me out."

She closed her eyes and felt herself sway. Instinctively her hands shot out to his chest; his heart pounded steady and strong against her palm. Maybe it was his heartbeat she had heard after all. No, no, it hadn't been.

"Melisande?" His face was hard, his breathing harsh.

She looked up at him, unsure of what she was about to say. The distant sound of car doors slamming made her start.

Cameron cursed beneath his breath. "It's the workmen, but I can tell them to go back home. Just tell me what you want." The phone began to ring out in the hallway. He ignored it. "Melisande?"

"I—I—"

"Tell me."

She averted her eyes from his. "I don't think you should tell them to go home."

He turned on his heel, strode into the hall, and jerked up the phone. "Yes?"

She could see him through the doorway, saw him listening to whoever was speaking to him, saw the granitelike expression, the hard glitter in his eyes. And she wondered how she would ever be able to tell him no . . . about anything.

"You're right," he said to whoever was on the other end of the line. "I'd forgotten." He drove stiffened fingers through his hair. "Okay, I'll be there in ten minutes." He slammed the phone back into its cradle and returned to the parlor. "I have an appointment in town. It's business, but I should be back in an hour. Will you still be here when I get back?"

She couldn't imagine having the strength to move. "I don't know."

"Yes or no, Melisande."

She couldn't tell him no. "Yes."

With a last searing look at her he snatched his

keys off the worktable and was gone. And with trembling limbs Melisande sank to the floor.

Melisande heard the men begin their work in various parts of the house, but she didn't move. It was as if that last look of Cameron's had rooted her to the spot, to the floor of the front parlor, to the town of Lacy, Alabama. What had started out to be a two-day trip—one day here, one day back—had stretched until now she was actually considering staying a week longer. Amazing.

She glanced vaguely around her, and her gaze fell on the wallpaper samples. She didn't have a clue how to begin decorating a house. Did you choose the paint colors first or the wallpaper? Or maybe you chose the upholstery fabric first. With a groan, she dropped her head into her hands. She couldn't coordinate her own clothes. Why was she even considering taking on this house as a project?

Cameron. It was Cameron of course.

He disturbed and threatened her, tantalized and excited. And no matter what he did or what he said, he always left her wanting more. . . .

The door opened, and Phyllis rushed in. "Cameron, I need to—" At the sight of Melisande sitting on the floor she came to a dead stop. "Oh, it's you."

Her expression wry, Melisande pushed herself up from the floor to her feet. "Yes, it's me. It's nice to see you again, Phyllis." Cameron's sister was wearing a crisp, orchid linen two-piece suit with matching bag and pumps and looked as fresh as a spring daffodil. In contrast, after sleeping all night in her clothes, Melisande looked as if she'd been trampled by not one, not two, not three, but a whole *herd* of elephants. And her hair needed gel in the worst way. She waited expectantly for Phyllis to make one of her "nice" pronouncements and tossed possible definitions around in her mind.

But much to her surprise Phyllis didn't seem to notice how she looked. In fact she seemed distracted. "Where's Cameron?"

"He had a business appointment in town. He said he'd be back in about an hour."

Phyllis touched her forehead, then tightly grasped her hands together. "Did he say who he was meeting?"

"No, I'm afraid he didn't."

Phyllis glanced at her watch. "What time did he leave?"

"Time?" Melisande went into a state of shock. She had no idea what time Cameron had left, she realized. "I didn't notice the time." It seemed impossible to her that those words had actually come from her mouth.

Phyllis nodded absently and wandered to a nearby window.

Still reeling from the fact that she hadn't monitored the time during the morning, Melisande frowned as she watched Phyllis. It took her a minute, but it finally dawned on her that Phyllis was upset about something that didn't have anything to do with her. "You could wait for him out on the porch if you like." She grimaced. Her suggestion sounded as if she had taken it upon herself to act as Cameron's hostess, when in fact her intention was to see if she could help Phyllis in some way. But Phyllis didn't seem to notice.

"I don't know," Phyllis said, wringing her hands.

"Would you like something to drink?" she asked.

Phyllis turned to look at her, but Melisande didn't think she saw her at all.

"Phyllis, is there something wrong?"

"No, nothing's wrong, I was just hoping to talk to Cameron."

"No one's hurt or sick, are they?"

Phyllis's laugh held an edge of hysteria.

Melisande went to her and took her arm. "Let's go into the kitchen. You can sit in there while you wait. I think I remember a bowl of lemons on the counter. I can make us some lemonade."

In the kitchen Melisande seated Phyllis, then stood back and eyed her lack of color with worry. Maybe a cup of hot tea would be better for her rather than something cold. She wished she knew. Since she had left home at the age of seventeen, the role of taking care of another person was unfamiliar to her. She didn't even take proper care of herself, much less anyone else.

Phyllis stirred and gazed up at her. "Why are you still here?"

Melisande smiled with relief. Phyllis was finally coming around. "'Here,' as in the kitchen? Or 'here,' as in Cameron's house?"

Phyllis slumped in the chair. "Forget I asked. It's none of my business anyway."

There was definitely something wrong. "I don't mind, really I don't. Cameron is your brother. I understand why you would want the best for him."

Phyllis dropped her head in her hands. "I do, but I don't have the right to meddle in his life when I've made such a mess of my own."

Melisande sank into a chair at a right angle to hers. "What's happened? Is it your husband? Cameron told me that you and your husband were having trouble."

Phyllis gave a short laugh and raised her head. Tears shimmered in her lovely blue eyes. "We're not having *trouble*. John would never even consider the possibility of our having trouble. That would be too vulgar. No, he simply ignores me, which is effortless for him since he spends as much time as possible away from our home."

"Have you tried to talk to him about it?"

"It's a little difficult to talk to him about anything when he leaves for the office every morning before I wake up and comes home after I've gone to sleep." A tear rolled down her cheek. She bit her lip. "So that means if I want to see him, I have to go to his office, which, by the way I did this morning. I decided to swallow my pride and ask him to go to lunch with me. I had planned to pack a picnic, like I used to before we were married, and take him to this special place we used to go . . ." Her voice trailed off.

"What happened?"

Her expression hardened. "Nothing. Not a thing. He said he had an important meeting and that he would see me at home tonight, and then he called in Janet, his secretary, and asked her to show me out."

"Did you tell him about your plans for the picnic?"

"I never got the chance."

Melisande reached out and touched Phyllis's arm. "I'm sorry. I've never been married, but I can imagine how much you must be hurting."

"I have been hurting, but I plan to quit as of now." Phyllis ran the back of her hand across her face, wiping away her tears. "I'm moving in with my friend Lisa. I've already packed a few bags. I'm on my way there now, but I wanted to come by and tell Cameron where I'd be."

"You're moving out? That's an awfully big step. Are you sure you should?"

"I should have done it weeks ago. Tell Cameron for me, will you?"

"I will, but I wish you'd wait and tell him yourself."

Phyllis shook her head and stood. "I think I'll feel better once I'm settled at Lisa's."

On impulse Melisande reached for her hand. "Stay with your friend for a few days, treat it like a little vacation. Maybe the distance will give you some perspective. But try not to do anything that you won't be able to undo. Cameron told me that you love your husband very much and that you've been married for ten years. I'm no expert, but it seems to me as if a love like that would be worth fighting for."

Phyllis smiled sadly. "Maybe that's the problem. Maybe I've never learned to fight."

"It's easy to learn. Trust me. I've fought for everything I've ever gotten in life."

"Do you always win?"

Melisande thought for a moment. "No, but I don't always lose either."

"You've been very kind to listen to me, Melisande. Tell Cameron I'll call him later."

When Cameron returned, he found Melisande behind the house on her hands and knees weeding the roses. He reached down for her and hauled her to her feet. "What are you doing out here? I told you I have some people coming to take care of this."

She brushed the dirt from her hands. "I needed something to do."

"I thought I'd left you with something to do. Remember the house?"

"Yeah, well, I said I'd be here when you got back, but I never agreed to decorate your house. I am glad I stayed, though."

"You are? Why?"

"Phyllis came by looking for you. She's moved out of her house and has gone to stay with Lisa."

He gave an exclamation. "Dammit, I was hoping it wouldn't come to this. What happened?" He listened while she told him everything Phyllis had said to her. "I'd better go over and see how she is."

She nodded. "I'm sure it will make her feel better to see you."

"It'll also make me feel better, although I don't know what I'll be able to do. I just wish I could talk her into returning to the house before John comes home and finds her gone."

"You must think a lot of John."

"I do. They're made for each other. Unfortunately they've both let other things come between them, and now they're going to have to decide what's most important to them." He hit a fisted hand into the palm of the other hand. "Dammit, it's hard to watch someone you love go through something so difficult."

"Yes, I suppose it would be." Even though she had a handful of close friends whom she would hate to see hurt for any reason, she wasn't sure she really knew what Cameron was going through. But she only had to look at him to know that he was suffering at the thought of his sister's heartache. And his suffering made her want to reach out and comfort him. She placed a hand on his arm. "She's going to be all right. Really, she will be. If she loves him, she'll move heaven and earth to save their marriage."

The blue of his eyes intensified. "Thank you for being here for her."

"Like I said, I'm glad I was." She glanced at her watch and frowned. Its alarm hadn't gone off once today, which meant she had missed at least two doses of antacid, not to mention her vitamins. He must have turned off all the alarm settings this morning. As soon as she got back to the house and located her purse, she'd better take a couple of antacid pills.

His long fingers circled her wrist, and his hand covered her watch, blocking her view of the time. "I can't go over to Lisa's until you tell me you're going to stay the week."

"Lisa's?" she asked, instantly diverted.

"That's where you said Phyllis is, didn't you?"

"Oh. Yes, I did." She remembered now. Lisa was the friend whom Phyllis had said she favored for him.

"Will you stay and help me with the decorating?"

She'd be a total fool to stay. "What about my business? What about the fact that I didn't bring but one other set of clothes with me? What about the fact that I couldn't decorate a barn much less a wonderful house like yours."

"What about the bed? What about the chance to spend more time together? What about being my date for the dance?"

She bent her head. *What about making a fool out of myself?*

He placed a knuckle beneath her chin and raised her face so he could see her eyes. "Melisande, sweet Melisande. You've heard all my arguments about why you should stay here. I've gone over and over them. Now I'm worried about my sister, but there's no way I'm going to leave you and go to her until you say you agree to my deal."

This was more than a simple business deal, *much* more, and they both knew it. She could tell herself all she wanted that the bed was her main motive for agreeing, but deep down she knew there was another, even more powerful reason, a reason she wasn't ready to look at yet or analyze. If she had any sense left at all, she would say—

"Yes." Her answer had escaped from her lips before she could stop it, and like a genie let out of a bottle, it couldn't be taken back.

His smile told her he had heard it. "Will you be here when I get back?"

A wave of panic swept over her, engulfing her with the unreasoning fear that she had just given part of herself away. "No." She shook her head firmly. "No. I have things I need to see about. I told you I'd stay, but that won't be possible if George Whitmark doesn't have a room he can rent me for that length of time."

"Getting a room at George's for a week won't be a problem. What else?"

The panic was mounting. "My work, my clothes, my *life* . . ."

He grasped her shoulders and bent close to her so that his face was level with hers. "Everything is going to work out fine, Melisande."

His voice was warm and soothing, but her nerves didn't settle, rather they tightened and twisted. His scent mingled with the fragrance of the roses and seeped into her pores. The intensity of his eyes penetrated straight through her.

"Go back to the motel, do what you have to do, then come back here. I'll try not to be long. Okay?"

Okay implied everything was right and sane and safe. But it wasn't. These last few days her world had tilted off its axis, and she had been thrown completely off balance.

"Melisande?"

"Okay." What else could she say? If she had said no, he wouldn't have left until she had agreed with him. Besides, agreeing to be here at the house when he returned put her in no more jeopardy than agreeing to stay a week had.

His long fingers threaded through her hair. "You know, I think your curls are relaxing." Then he pressed a warm kiss to her lips and strode away.

"Glad to hear you're going to stay another week," George said to Melisande later that afternoon. "I've never had anyone staying here be less trouble than you. I don't even have to make up your bed."

A flush of color came up beneath her skin. "Yes, well, if you're sure you can spare the cabin."

"It and eight more if you want them."

"Thanks, but all I need is one."

"Then I'll be getting back to work." George touched the brim of his cap and sauntered down the row of cabins to Cabin 3, where he was still working.

Melisande rolled her eyes and entered Cabin 6, which she had just reserved for the next week. George must have known she didn't return to the motel last night, and she was sure he had jumped to the same conclusion everyone else would when they heard about it—that she had spent the night with Cameron. And she couldn't even deny it.

The next week might get pretty interesting. For the first time in her life she was in danger of having a reputation as a scarlet woman. She supposed it wouldn't be so bad if she deserved the reputation, but she didn't. And though she couldn't quite put her finger on it, somehow that thought was terribly depressing.

She placed a call to Sam, who was delighted by her decision, but told her in no uncertain terms that he would quit if she checked in with him twice a day. He wanted her to rest. She didn't believe his threat, but prudently decided to limit her calls to one a day. Then she dialed Noelle's number.

"Noelle?"

"Hi, Mel. What's up?"

Melisande smiled. It was reassuring to hear Sam and Noelle call her Mel. Talking to them was like a touchstone with her world, the *real* world.

Noelle continued without giving her a chance to answer. "I called your office yesterday, and Sam told me you were on a quest for a bed."

"That's pretty much it. And what's more, my quest is being extended to a week and I'm stuck in Alabama with only two changes of clothes, neither one of which you would approve."

"Good grief, why didn't you call me sooner?"

"Because I kept thinking I could wind things up and come home. But it turns out the one bed in the world in which I can sleep is owned by a man who can't make up his mind whether to sell it to me, and no matter how hard I've tried, I haven't been able to hurry his decision."

"What is he? Some kind of creep?"

"Believe me, there are a great many words that could be used for him, but *creep* isn't one of them."

"How very interesting. Tell me more."

"Maybe when I get home." But she knew she wouldn't tell anyone about Cameron. How could she? What was between her and Cameron couldn't be interpreted or explained, not even to herself. "Listen, could you go over to my house, grab a few casual outfits out of my closet, and express them to me? I also need underwear and shoes . . . oh, and I guess I'm going to need makeup too. I've got to attend something called a Founders Day Dance."

"No kidding? Well, in that case you're going to need a dress."

She groaned. "Shoot. I hadn't thought about it, but I guess I am."

"Do you have anything in particular in mind?"

"No, not really. I'll rely on your judgment as usual. But . . ."

"Yes?"

"But make it a really *spectacular* dress. These people haven't seen me in anything but jeans, and as long as I'm going to show up at the affair, it would be nice if I could knock their socks off."

"Now you're talking, and I know just the dress. It's brand-new in the shop. Leave everything to me. Just give me the address where you want it sent."

Melisande had been back at the house for over an hour when the phone rang. She hesitated, but then quickly decided that people would be no more scandalized by the fact that she answered Cameron's phone than the fact that she had spent the night with him.

She picked up the phone. "Hello."

"Hi."

At the sound of Cameron's voice, something warm and liquid curled through her lower body. "Hi. How's Phyllis?"

"Stubborn and determined and very, very hurt."

"I'm sorry."

He sighed. "So am I, but having you there waiting for me is making this a lot easier."

She shrugged off the compliment. "I said I'd be here."

"What have you been doing?"

"I spent most of the afternoon at the motel, but now I'm sitting out on the porch looking at Aunt Sarah's roses."

"What else?"

"Nothing."

"Nothing?"

"Not really."

"Okay, well it sounds like a nice way to pass the time. Would you mind doing it a little longer? I'm going to stop by John's on the way home and talk to him. I'm sure he's every bit as upset as Phyllis."

"No problem."

"Good. Why don't you check the refrigerator, see what looks appetizing to you, and fix yourself something to eat?"

"But what about you? When are you going to eat?"

"Lisa's fed me."

"Oh." Elizabeth baked homemade bread, and Mary Ann baked heavenly pecan pies. More than likely Lisa routinely and superbly turned out twelve-course dinners.

"I'll see you in a little bit."

"Right."

She hung up and stared at the roses. She supposed she should do something productive, like make an effort to decide on some sort of decorating plan for the house. Or perhaps she might do a little more weeding. She could even take Cameron's suggestion and eat. She could, but she didn't feel like it. She had no appetite, and her stomach hurt a little, a strange empty, aching feeling.

She rubbed at the crystal face of her watch, realizing she had forgotten to take her antacids. She needed to reset her alarms, and she would. Soon. But first she would sit here a little while longer.

Cameron was at Lisa's house. She had cooked him dinner and had given his sister a place to stay. He was probably very grateful, and Phyllis obviously liked her. Maybe Cameron would end up marrying Lisa.

Melisande made a face. It was only natural that she be mildly curious about whom he would end up with, she told herself, but somehow she couldn't get enthused about Lisa for him. Since she had never met the woman, it was an unfair judgment on her part, but that's just the way it was.

Shadows lengthened, the light faded. She continued to gaze at the roses. Their lush beauty and their heady perfume enthralled her. Sometime in the evening she rose from her chair and went down to cut a bouquet for Cameron's bedroom.

Seven

Sunlight slanted across Melisande's eyes. Moving her head fretfully, she tried to escape the light so that she could sink back down into the soft, enveloping cloud of blissful sleep. But the light persisted, shining against the back of her lids, dragging her up through feathery layers of comfort. She smelled roses and some other wonderfully compelling and enticing scent. The scent tugged and pulled at her, willing her to wakefulness. With a contented stretch, she opened her eyes and saw Cameron.

He was lying close beside her, propped up on his elbow, gazing steadily down at her. "Good morning."

A violent tremor rocked through her nervous system. She had come up out of a deep sleep to find herself in bed with the very man who had filled her dreams during the night. The situation was charged with a provocative intimacy.

Then a further realization hit her, and she groaned. "I did it again, didn't I?"

He nodded. "You were asleep when I got home. You slept like a baby all night long."

His hair looked in need of a comb, his jaw in need of a razor, but he still managed to steal her breath away. He was all hard muscle and potent masculinity, and at this moment she felt extremely vulnerable. "You slept here in the bed all night, didn't you?"

A trace of grimness entered his expression. "I wouldn't say I got much sleep, but, yes, Melisande, I was beside you all night."

The thought sent heat flashing to her lower body. In a useless, but instinctively protective gesture, she pressed her hand to her belly and encountered silky material. Her mind scrambled to process the information. Her shorts were gone, and she was wearing only her panties and—she looked down—her bra.

With a gasp she snatched the sheet up to her neck. "You undressed me?" Her tone was filled with both accusation and disbelief.

"Yes." His eyes glittered darkly. "I thought it would be a shame if you had to sleep in your clothes two nights in a row. And also . . . I flat couldn't resist. If I couldn't make love to you, I at least wanted to be able to feel your skin against mine."

Despite the heat inside her she shivered. "You—"

"That's right, Melisande. I held you all night long. I watched you sleep, and I watched you dream." His lips twitched with self-deprecating humor. "And like I said, I somehow even managed to get a little sleep myself."

For an unguarded instant she wished she had been awake so that she could have remembered the night. But she had spent the long, dark hours in a deep, velvet sleep that had been filled with shadowy erotic dreams of Cameron. In the dreams she had felt his hair-roughened chest against her skin, the strength of his arms around her, the hardness of his arousal. . . . And she had snuggled against him, reveling in the heat of his body, safe in the knowledge that it was only a dream.

His eyes stayed on her as he combed his fingers through her hair. "I could have made love to you in the night, and you would have thought it was a dream."

Once again he had seen straight through her. "I think I would have woken up," she said, reaching for sarcasm, but finding only a bald yearning. The idea of waking up with him inside her depleted her strength and started an aching throb in her loins.

Suddenly and with barely contained violence, he rolled out of bed. Her gaze followed him, her eyes wide, her heartbeat wild and erratic. Standing in the morning sunlight, wearing only white knit briefs, with his blatant arousal pressing against them, he literally made her mouth water.

Sunlight gilded the muscles and planes of his body. He looked hard, intense, and near the end of his rope with her. "I told you I'd leave it up to you, and I'm trying like hell to keep my word, but you need to know, Melisande—all I can think about anymore is what it would be like to feel your nipple harden in my mouth, sink into your tight heat, and have you milk me dry with those tiny muscles you have inside you.

A sensual haze of heat came down around her, surrounding her, threatening to suffocate her with desire. She couldn't move, couldn't speak, couldn't do a thing to stop him when he turned on his heel and headed for the bathroom.

"I've got to have a cold shower or I'm not going to

be responsible for what happens next," he muttered, disappearing through the door.

She lay where she was, drawing deep, searing breaths into her lungs. He was gone, she told herself. He was not only out of the bed, he was out of the room. She was safe. But she felt no relief. She had awakened from a series of soft, erotic dreams to find herself abruptly plunged into the blazing reality of scalding passion.

She gathered her strength and pushed herself upward until she was upright and cushioned against a mound of pillows. Listening, she heard the shower running in the bathroom. The cold water would quench his desire for her, but what, she wondered helplessly, would quench her desire for him?

Time passed. She heard the shower shut off and him moving around in the bathroom, and still she was unable to answer her question. Or move. She was trapped in the fiery grip of an out-of-control delirium, and she didn't know how to escape. Her body was dictating to her mind. She felt hollow and achy, and all she could think about was how much she wanted him, had wanted him in fact from the beginning. When he walked back into the room, she stared, her eyes hungry, her body in pain.

A towel was knotted around his lean waist, leaving his chest and shoulders bare. His hair lay wetly against his head, his brown skin gleamed with moisture, and drops of water glistened in the thicket of dark curls that grew across his broad, muscled chest.

"What are you still doing in bed?" he asked roughly. "I would have thought you were the type to hit the floor running in the morning."

"I am. Usually."

He cocked his head to one side, studying her. Then showing no embarrassment that only a towel covered him, he strolled to the end of the bed. "So what's different about this morning, Melisande?"

"I'm not sure." But she was sure. The difference was the fever that had risen in her body, a scorching fever that raged for him.

His brows drew together over intense, darkly blue eyes. "Do you feel all right?"

"Yes." *No.* She felt strange, edgy, supersensitive to even the air that touched her skin. She was in agony, and she was very much afraid that only he could help her.

He gazed at her for a long moment, and his voice softened. "You look wonderful. Sleep becomes you. But—"

He moved around the bed to her, bringing his clean soap, water, and tantalizing man scent with him. She swallowed in an effort to relieve the dryness of her throat.

"There's something going on with you," he said, his heated-molasses voice husky and low. "What is it?"

She knew what it was, but she couldn't tell him. It was the desire that was pounding through her bloodstream at an ever-increasing pace. She gritted her teeth together to keep from blurting out the truth. Sweat broke out on her brow from the effort.

He dropped to the bed, reached out, and touched the clenched muscle in her jaw. "What is it?" he asked thickly. "What's wrong?"

She closed her eyes and shook her head.

"Is there something you'd like to tell me, Melisande?" He waited, his fingers massaging the tightness of her jaw.

She knew her silence would do her no good. She

knew that he would eventually see into her, see what she was doing her best to hide, see her need and longing. And she wasn't wrong.

His fingers traced the contours of her face as if he were blind and was reading her with the tips of his fingers. But he wasn't blind, and he could read her better than anyone ever had.

His breathing deepened, became rough and heavy. "Do you want me to make love to you, Melisande? Is that what you want to tell me?"

The breath lodged in her throat, her heartbeat suspended. Then she felt his fingers leave her face and trail down her throat, leaving fire in their wake.

"Do you like the way I make you feel?" His fingers stopped briefly over her rapidly beating pulse point, then stroked on to her lacy bra. "Do you like it when I touch your breasts?" His fingers lightly traced the lace edge of the bra, heating her skin and her mind until she feared for her sanity.

"Talk to me, honey. Tell me what it is you want."

Her lashes fluttered up, and she met his gaze square on, revealing the truth and her soul to him.

He drew a quick indrawn breath.

"Yes." Her voice was choked and barely above a whisper. "Oh, Lord, yes."

He gripped her face between his hands. "Say it louder. Say what I want to hear."

"I want you. I want you to make love to me."

With a muttered oath he stripped the sheet from her and pulled her into his arms for a kiss that scorched her with the fire he had been holding back.

Emotions of all sorts exploded inside him. Melisande had brought him to his knees, but now he was about to make her his. For all he knew, it might even be the other way around, but he didn't care.

She wound her arms around his neck, giving herself up to the kiss and the passion. Her hunger had burned straight through her and out into the open for him to see. Now she wanted to sate her needs and longings, fill herself up on his taste. And her only thought was to wonder why she had waited so long.

He had been up-front with her, telling her almost from the first that he wanted her. Why couldn't she have been as up-front with him? Why had she denied herself so long? If there were reasons, she couldn't recall a single one.

Somehow she found herself on her back, lying crosswise over the bed, with him above her. Her panties and bra were gone, as was his towel. As was any thought of polite restraint.

Powerless against her need for him, she held out her arms, and he went to her.

His tongue, hot and moist, sought out her secret hollows and hidden valleys. His love for her made what was about to happen precious to him. He wanted to savor every beautiful moment. At the same time a deep, primitive hunger inside him was firing his blood and driving him on. He wasn't sure he was going to be able to wait much longer.

She arched and shifted, offering herself to him without embarrassment or reserve. There wasn't time or space for either emotion. The fondling of his hand, the stroking of his tongue, the caress of his mouth were filling her with pure unadulterated pleasure. His demands were exhausting, and at the same time exhilarating. She didn't think it possible for her to absorb any more. But she was wrong.

With his tongue he made long, deep, gliding

forays into places never before explored. She was shocked; she was on fire; she was in need so great she thought she might die of it. Violent tremors shook her, and slowly, steadily, the pressure inside her became unbearable.

He moved over her and thrust deeply into her, and whole other worlds of ecstasy opened up in her. He moved in and out of her with a hard, savage tempo that sent great waves of fiery sensation rolling through her.

She drew her knees up, placing her feet flat on the bed, and her hands reached down and grasped his tightly muscled buttocks, urging him deeper into her. With each thrust of his loins the rippling and flexing of his iron-hard muscles thrilled her, and a gasping cry tore from her throat.

He responded, hammering more powerfully into her. Her hips rose time after time, arching up to meet him, demanding fulfillment. She had never known lovemaking could be like this, fiery, consuming, and sweetly and utterly insane.

He clasped her hips, welding her to him. The heat built in her, completely possessing her, until finally, with a wild, indecipherable sound, she crested in a shimmering and powerful release that went on and on. She clung to him, feeling for that one unbelievable moment as if she were truly a part of him.

The mid-morning breeze flirted with the lace curtains at the windows, sending their hems fluttering. Cameron held Melisande in his arms, her back curved against his chest and thighs, spoon fashion.

"Don't regret what just happened between us," he murmured, his mouth close to her ear.

"I'm not. How could I?"

He laughed softly, his breath blowing a tendril of her hair. "But you are. I can almost feel you tensing, muscle by muscle. What's wrong?"

It was useless for her to say *nothing* again. He wouldn't believe her, and neither would she. She was frightened, but of what she didn't know. She had the frantic urge to retreat, an almost impossible task considering that she was lying naked in his bed within the circle of his arms. She was surrounded by him, his body, the musk and sex smell of him. She had to do something.

Anchoring the sheet beneath her arms, she eased from his hold and put a small amount of distance between them. Propping herself up with pillows, she mentally searched for the mundane to use as a buffer against him. "It's quiet, too quiet. Where are the workmen?"

"I gave them the day off so that you and I could have time alone."

Her teeth came together. "Why? Did you actually *anticipate* what just happened between us?"

"Come on, Melisande. You know better than that."

She did and she didn't. Her fingers sought out the familiar, comforting feel of the crystal face of her watch, but didn't find it. She glanced down at her bare wrist. "Where's my watch?"

"On the nightstand beside you."

With the same urgency she would use if she were reaching for a lifeline, she reached for the watch and slid it onto her wrist. "The alarm system seems to have stopped working."

"I turned it off."

She had already guessed as much. "You shouldn't have done that. Without those alarms I won't remember when to take my antacids."

"Do you need them?"

"*Yes*, I do." Her hand automatically went to her stomach, and suddenly she couldn't remember the last time her stomach had hurt. "Look, Cameron," she said, turning back to him. "I don't want you jumping to any conclusions because of what just happened between us. Things can't become serious between us. I have a career that's very important to me."

Stretched out in all his naked male splendor, he casually lifted an eyebrow. "If anyone's jumping to conclusions, it just might be you."

"What do you mean?"

"Have I asked you for anything more than a week?"

His statement should have relaxed her, but instead she found herself tensing more. "No . . ."

"What's worrying you, Melisande? What's *really* worrying you?"

Good question, she thought .The power of their lovemaking had astonished her and had given her undreamed-of pleasure. And because of it she was scared to death. When she had walked into this house that twilight evening four days ago, she had had her life all mapped out and under control. Up to that point she had prided herself on always making rational, logical decisions.

But her decision to make love to Cameron had been neither. In one totally illogical, irrational moment she had surrendered to the physical.

The sex between them had been incredible, but it was over now, and a strong sense of self-preservation was urging her to pick up what was left of herself and continue on with her life as she always had—before she lost that life altogether.

Cameron observed the inner turmoil written on her face with trepidation. He had accomplished quite a bit in the last few days. He had gotten her to relax degree by degree, and to consent to stay for a week. She had even had two good nights' sleep in a row. And miracle of miracles, they had made love. In fact he wanted her again right now with a ferocity that amazed him. But he wanted much more than sexual gratification from her. He wanted her to love him as much as he loved her.

It wasn't going to be easy. Even as he lay there wanting her, loving her, she was trying to reason out what had just happened between them so that she could put it behind her. He refused to let that happen.

He shifted nearer. "You know what?" he whispered. "You're thinking so hard, I can actually hear your brain clicking furiously away."

Her solemn thoughts dissolved at the sight of the irresistible humor flickering in his eyes. "Really? I would have thought all this hair of mine would have muffled the sound." Self-consciously she took two handfuls of hair and pulled it back in an effort at containment.

With a grin he drew her hands down, freeing her hair to return to its coiled turbulence. "All that hair of yours fascinates me."

"Well, it irritates me. I've never had a day that wasn't a bad hair day." She blinked. "Wait a minute. I started out telling you that our relationship couldn't be serious and now we're talking about my hair?"

He twirled a curl around his finger. "Relax, Melisande. Stop fighting and just enjoy."

"I will. I am. It's just that sex is a complication I didn't need or want, Cameron."

"Why look on it as a complication?"

Because she was lying in bed with him, naked, feeling tinglingly alive from their lovemaking, and all she could think of was that she wanted more. "Because it's bound to interfere with our working relationship this next week."

He tugged on her sheet, pulling it down to her waist. "So what? It'll be a good type of interference, the *best*."

She swallowed hard and plucked unsuccessfully at the sheet. "You don't understand. Having sex with a man is not something I do on a regular basis."

"You can't imagine how glad I am to hear that."

The possessiveness in his tone had her turning her head so she could look at him. Had she really heard it, or had she been mistaken?

His eyes twinkled as he smiled at her. His hand cupped a breast caressingly and his palm gently scraped back and forth across her nipple. "Are you hungry?"

"Hungry?" Her insides were heating. Inhaling deeply, she slid down in the bed so that her face was even with his. She breathed in the fragrance of his skin and ran her hand along the smooth skin of cheek. "You know something?"

"I can't imagine."

"I've just figured out how I would advertise the way you smell."

"You'd advertise the way I smell?" He leaned over and kissed her nipple, encompassing it within the moistness of his mouth and lightly scraping it with his teeth.

She moaned and lifted his head. "If you want to hear this, you're going to have to stop that."

He chuckled huskily. "Okay, I'm listening."

"Right from the first I've felt that if I could just distill your scent into words, I could make a fortune."

"And you have?"

"I've decided that words, no matter what the combination, would be hopelessly inadequate, but at least I've figured out what the campaign should be." She stroked her thumb across his moist bottom lip, and her voice was soft and somewhat raspy. "I'd run your picture, wearing very little but the cologne I was trying to sell, and beneath your picture I would say:

"*Ladies, wouldn't you just love to have him for dinner? Invite him over and splash the cologne on him. Afterward you can even go out to eat. You can, that is, if you're still hungry.*"

His eyes darkened, and with a groan he yanked her to him.

When they finally got around to eating, it was lunchtime. Afterward Melisande placed a phone call to George and discovered her clothes had arrived.

She hung up the hallway phone to find Cameron standing in the parlor doorway watching her. "I've had some clothes sent to the motel. I'm going to run over there, take a shower, and change."

His first instinct was not to let her out of his sight. "What's wrong with what you have on?"

"Nothing," she said wryly, "except that when I take it off, I may burn it."

His gaze roamed hungrily over her. The jean shorts and T-shirt left her legs and arms bare. She had managed to secure most of her hair with a rubber band, but already several independent-minded strands had sprung free. And only a faint hint of the shadows remained beneath her eyes. She looked adorable and incredibly sexy. "Why don't you just bring everything back over here?"

"You mean move in?" she asked slowly.

"Why not? You know you're going to be spending the nights here anyway."

Anger flared quick and hot. "You have no right to presume such a thing." The minute she said it, she knew that he did. The way she turned fiery and wild every time he pulled her to him gave him every right. And the knowledge didn't make her any less angry.

He held up his hands in a placating gesture. "Okay, I shouldn't have said it like that. Forgive me. But tell me something—are you really going back to the motel at nights and a bed you can't sleep in, when you could be here with me and the bed you can actually get a good night's sleep in?"

"Why shouldn't I?"

"Because you won't sleep."

That was true.

"And because I can't stand to be without you."

She flushed, heat climbing up her neck to her face. "Everyone will talk about us if I move in here with you."

"Maybe a few people will, but why should you care? You don't know them."

"Maybe not, but you do."

"And I don't give a damn."

She exhaled a long breath. She wanted very badly to stay here with him, she realized. In fact she'd be miserable if she went back to the motel cabin at night. "I'll bring a few of my things over," she said guardedly. "But I'm going to keep the cabin." The cabin represented a modicum of independence, which was very important to her.

"Fine," Cameron said, more than satisfied. And his first instinct not to let her out of his sight held. "I'll come with you."

Eight

Her lovely face marred with a frown, Phyllis leaned back in the rattan chair next to her brother's. "If John thinks a bouquet of flowers can make up for months of neglect, he'd better think again."

Cameron sipped his coffee and watched Melisande as she wandered among the rosebushes in front of the house. Now and then she would stop to finger one delicate petal, and he wondered what she was thinking. She had changed into a turquoise and blue cotton-knit short set at the motel, and she had made another attempt to subdue her hair, pulling it back and tying it at the nape of her neck with a turquoise scarf. Already wisps of curls blew free. He was rooting for the hair.

"John had to do something, Sis. You wouldn't take his calls, and when he showed up at Lisa's door, you wouldn't let him in."

"Of course I wouldn't. I gave him plenty of chances before I moved out. Now the next time I see him I want it to be in divorce court."

Her radical statement drew Cameron's attention away from Melisande. "You don't mean that."

"I wouldn't have said it if I didn't. Whose side are you on, anyway?"

"Do you even have to ask?"

With a sigh, she rubbed her forehead. "I'm sorry, Cameron. I didn't sleep well last night."

"I can imagine, but if it's any comfort, I'm willing to bet John didn't either."

"If he didn't, I can assure you it wasn't because of me. More than likely he was just working, and probably it was with that new secretary of his."

"Come on, Phyllis. You've got to know there isn't anything going on between John and his secretary."

"Do I?"

"Yes, you do. I doubt if he even sees her as a woman. She's simply someone who follows his instructions to the letter. Right?"

Reluctantly she nodded, then added with real feeling, "If I actually thought he was fooling around with his secretary, I wouldn't divorce him, I'd *kill* him."

Cameron grinned. Whether she knew it or not, she still loved her husband. "That's my girl." His gaze returned to the bright splash of color in the garden. "Melisande," he called, "come and join us. The ice is going to melt in your tea."

Melisande lifted her hand to shield her eyes from the sun and gazed uncertainly at the porch. "Are you sure?" Even though Cameron had insisted on her joining him and his sister, she had been reluctant. In an effort to give them privacy she had excused herself and drifted down to the rosebushes.

Phyllis beckoned to her with a weary gesture. "You might as well come sit down, Melisande. I'm not talking about anything important. Just my Type A–personality husband." Her voice dropped in tone. "Or I guess I should say, my Type A–almost-*ex*-husband."

Melisande sat down at the table and looked at Cameron. His blue eyes were shadowed with worry, and it wrenched her heart. She cast around in her mind for something she could do to help him. "I'm sorry, Phyllis, but I couldn't help but overhear you say something about divorce?"

"There's nothing else to be done."

"That's not true, Sis."

Melisande could see that Phyllis wasn't buying what Cameron was trying so hard to sell. But there was more than one way to sell a product, the product in this case being Phyllis and John's marriage. "Then again, maybe it *is* true. Maybe divorce is the only answer." Two pairs of blue eyes focused on her. She cleared her throat. "But even so, you do need to talk to John. The two of you have things you've got to decide, such as how you're going to divide up your property."

Cameron sat forward. "Melisande—"

Ignoring Cameron's warning tone, she continued. "For instance, you'll have to decide how you're going to divide the silver."

Phyllis's eyes widened with distressed. "But we couldn't divide the silver. We picked out the pattern together. It's Grand Baroque, and we both love it."

"Well, then maybe he'll say you can have it, and then you could give him the china."

The furrows between her brows deepened. "But the china and the silver are a perfect complement for each other. We planned it that way."

"In that case one of you could keep both the china and the silver and the other could have, say, the bedroom furniture, or even the living room furniture."

Phyllis made a distressed sound. "We picked out everything together, we planned our house, its furnishings, our future. We were going to have children. . . ."

Melisande stole a glance at Cameron. He had sat back and was watching her with interest. "Listen, Phyllis, you mustn't think of divorce as an end to something, but rather as a beginning. You'll be on your own and can live your life exactly as you want. You just have to make sure that you don't repeat the same mistake. Remain alone, live your own life, on your own."

"Alone?"

"Absolutely. See, it's this way." Her tone dropped confidentially. "A man is like a pot of honey. He might look tempting and sweet and you might want to dip in for a taste, but remember that once you do, you're stuck."

Phyllis blinked. Cameron's eyes narrowed.

Maybe, Melisande thought, it was time to back off a little and try another tack. "Did you say John's a Type A?"

"More like a Type A *Plus,*" Phyllis murmured. "Either that or he's working all those hours in order to avoid me."

Cameron reached over and covered his sister's hand with his. "Now, you know that's not true."

"How would I know that?" For a moment she looked as if she might burst into tears.

The helpless expression on Cameron's face compelled Melisande to speak. "He wouldn't have sent you the flowers if that was the case."

"You don't understand. He sent the flowers because it was the *proper, expected* thing for him to do. He always sent me flowers on our anniversary, too, but it wasn't a big deal. All he has to do is ask his secretary to place the order."

"Was there a card with the flowers and did it have a personal message?"

Phyllis's hand gestured dismissively. "He asked me to dinner, but our problem has been building for months. A bouquet of flowers and a dinner aren't going to fix it."

"Then what will?"

Phyllis's stern expression crumpled. "I don't know."

Cameron squeezed her hand reassuringly. "Having dinner with him would be a start, Sis. If nothing else, it would give you a chance to tell him exactly how you've felt all these months. You've complained that he won't listen to you. Well, now he's saying he will."

"I'm not sure listening and talking are possible for us anymore. Somewhere along the way we've forgotten how."

"You can relearn. And dinner would give him a chance to present his side," Melisande added, wondering with amazement how she had ever fallen into the role of marriage counselor. Never in the history of the world had there been anyone less qualified than she.

"He doesn't have a *side*," Phyllis said bitterly.

Melisande's heart went out to her. She had never known love between a man and a woman, so she could only imagine the pain of having a love like that end. "I don't know your husband, but I do know a little bit about Type A personalities, and you have to understand. They love to work so much, it's hard for them to stop." She was using *they*, but she realized she could just as easily be using *we*. "There's this terrific need inside to prove something, and the need never goes away." She glanced at Cameron and saw that she had his undivided attention. His unwavering gaze made her uncomfortable; but in this instance it was Phyllis's attention she wanted, and she had it.

"What is it they're trying to prove?"

Melisande shrugged. "Sometimes it's just that they need to prove to themselves that they're capable of succeeding."

"But John has already succeeded. He's one of Alabama's foremost attorneys."

Melisande wasn't sure what to say next. Her explanation made sense to her, but she realized she hadn't given Phyllis the reassurance she needed. Her little speech had accomplished one thing, though. It had struck home with a vengeance. Her belief that a single life was best for people like her had been reinforced. With her own words she had condemned herself to a life without a loving, lasting relationship.

Just then the phone rang. Cameron excused himself and went into the house.

Phyllis glanced around her. "I've just noticed. It's so quiet here today. Where are the workmen?"

Melisande tried without success to control a blush. "Cameron gave them the day off."

Melisande and Phyllis heard his voice through the screen door as he answered the phone.

"Hello? Yes, Elizabeth?" His voice carried more than a hint of impatience. "No. I told you last night I won't be able to do anything . . . I'm sorry, but I'm just not interested. . . ."

Melisande cringed with embarrassment for Elizabeth. She knew it was another whiplike reversal of decision, but she couldn't help but feel sorry for her.

Listening to her brother, Phyllis sighed heavily. "I should never have tried to interfere in Cameron's life. I thought he needed someone, and then"—she shrugged, a vaguely puzzled expression in her eyes—"you just appeared out of no-where."

Melisande gave her a small, tight smile. "Don't worry about it. I'll disappear again in a few days, and then I'm sure he'll become interested in one of your friends." In trying to reassure Phyllis, she had just made herself thoroughly depressed.

Phyllis leaned forward. "Please don't be hurt by what I said. I want Cameron to be happy, it's all I ever wanted. And if you're the one he wants . . ."

"He doesn't. At least not in the long-term way you mean."

"I'm not so sure."

"I am." Why was she feeling such pain? she wondered. Her first thought was that she needed to take her antacid tablets, but then she realized it wasn't her stomach that was hurting. "Things will work out for both you and Cameron, Phyllis. You're both going to be happy, you'll see. But you need to give John another chance. Go to dinner with him tonight. Talk to him. Sometimes, people get so caught up in their day-to-day living that they lose sight of what's important to them."

"Thanks for talking to Phyllis," Cameron said. He had just seen Phyllis off and had come back into the house to find Melisande sitting cross-legged on the floor of the front parlor, delving through the boxes of fabric samples.

"It was no big deal." She wished he would go away. She didn't want to be with him or with anyone. The pain she had experienced when she had talked to Phyllis about Cameron had lingered, putting her in an extremely bad mood.

"Yes, it was a big deal. It was also very nice of you."

"I don't know. I'm not sure I was any help."

"I think you were. At least she agreed to *think* about going out to dinner with John tonight. Before, she was adamant that she wouldn't." He paused. "Do you really believe what you said about people getting so caught up in their day-to-day living that they lose sight of what's important to them?"

"Sure. I think it's probably easy for something like that to happen."

"Has it ever happened to you?"

She shook her head. "I always remember what's important."

"And what's that?"

She studied a fabric swatch with frowning concentration. "My career." She was the Type A personality she had talked to Phyllis about. She would never be able to fall in love and have a home and a family like a normal person. She didn't know anything about putting balance in her life or compromising with another person. And she was only just beginning to realize how sad it was.

"Has that always been the case?"

"Always," she said firmly.

"How long is that?"

The question caught her attention. Bewildered, she looked at him. "You're asking me how long is *always*?"

"I'm asking you exactly how long you've wanted your career? From the moment you were born?"

"No, not exactly . . ."

"Then how long?"

She felt her nerves tightening. "What difference does it make, Cameron?"

"None. So tell me." His gaze went to her jaw line, where a muscle flexed as she unconsciously gritted her teeth, then it returned to her eyes.

"I'm not sure I remember the exact moment."

"The general moment will do."

Why was he being so persistent? she wondered, irritated. She deliberately turned her back on him and began pawing through a box of color samples. "I was young. Very young."

She fell silent, and for a moment he didn't think she was going to say anything more. But she did.

"I spent six weeks here the summer I was eight, except that I was supposed to have spent the whole summer. My mother had been sick, and it was Aunt Sarah's way of giving my mother a break." She paused and swallowed. "One day Aunt Sarah came to find me. I was down by the river playing. She said my dad had called and wanted me to come home early. I was sorry to leave Aunt Sarah, but I was thrilled to be going back home. I thought Dad's call meant he and Mom had missed me. Anyway Aunt Sarah put me on the bus that day. We lived in northern Alabama then. . . ."

"What happened?" He had quietly circled the room so that he could see her face. Vulnerability was written all over her; he felt as if someone had punched him in the stomach.

She stared unseeingly into the box. "When I got home, my dad told me my mother had died. He comforted me that day, but immediately after the funeral he started to drink, and he didn't stop until he died almost ten years later."

"I'm so sorry, Melisande." And he was. So much so, he could feel the pain of the eight-year-old little girl she had been. "It sounds as if you had to pretty much raise yourself."

She grabbed up a handful of loose color cards, then let them trickle through her fingers. "I tried to help him. I tried really hard, but he didn't want to be helped. I never gave up on him, but he gave up on himself."

"It must have been a lonely life for you."

A muscle along her jaw line flexed once again, but she didn't confirm or contradict what he had said. "I was busy. I turned my attention to the future and did everything I could to ensure that I'd be able to get out of that town as soon as possible and achieve a decent life of my own."

"Did you get a scholarship to college?"

She nodded. "And when my dad died, I left and never looked back. What do you think of this color?" She held up a pale rose fabric sample.

He barely noticed she had something in her hand, he was focusing so hard on her and what she had told him. "You've come a long way, Melisande. You ought to be very proud of yourself."

"Proud?" The word struck her as odd. She glanced at him and was surprised to see him so close.

"You've accomplished a great deal. Don't you think you can slow down a little now?"

A tightness gripped her chest. She forced her attention back to the paint sample. "I can't. I might lose everything I've worked so hard for."

"You can't lose what you've already accomplished."

It did make a certain amount of sense, but she still wasn't sure, and besides, she didn't want to talk about herself any longer. She had told him things that people who had known her for years didn't even know. She held up the sample again. "You didn't tell me what you think of this color?"

"It's fine." He came down on his haunches beside her. "Melisande, haven't you heard of having it all? You can, you know. You can have your career and a life outside it. A family. It's just a matter of dividing your time differently."

A scene flashed into her mind of her coming home from work and laughing children running into her arms. And behind them her husband stood, smiling lovingly at her. *Cameron*. She mutely shook her head.

"What are you afraid of, Melisande? Of losing part of yourself? You won't. All your hard work will still mean something."

Minutes before, she had wanted him to go away, but now with him so close, she only wanted him to change the subject. "I'm not sure what your point is," she said carefully. "Why this sudden interest in my life?"

His need to tell her he loved her was growing by the minute, but he knew she wasn't ready to hear it. He lightly brushed his fingers across her lips. "I have this bad habit. Once I get a woman in my bed, I tend to try to organize her life."

She found she didn't like the idea of the other women who had graced his bed in the past, not even a little bit. "I see. And have many women found their way into your bed?"

His lips spread into a seductively charming smile. "Only one so far."

She didn't believe him for a minute, but it made her feel better that he had lied. "And how did you do with organizing her life?"

"So far not so great."

"Well, you can't win every time."

He leaned down and lightly touched his mouth to hers. "How about this once?"

A thrill shot through her. She laughed softly. "Not a chance." She put her hands on his shoulders and pushed, sending him sprawling onto his backside. "Now may I have your attention please?"

"If my attention hasn't been on you," he said wryly, shifting and straightening until his back was against a wall and one knee was raised, "then kindly tell me where you think it's been."

"It's been on me, but the wrong parts of me."

"As far as I've been able to tell, there are no wrong parts of you."

The huskiness of his tone was almost her undoing. "Try to pay attention, Cameron. I'm about to tell you how I've decided your house should be decorated. Are you interested?"

"As long as you're no farther than arm's length away from me, I'm interested."

As difficult as it was, she ignored his comment. "Okay, here it is. I think the key to the house's color scheme should be Aunt Sarah's roses. You can't look out a window, front or back, without seeing them. They're everywhere, and they're beautiful. Why not bring their colors in? We could use the palest and softest of their colors for the background and then their brightest colors for accent. In another words, we'd be using soft roses and pinks, the pure whites and the lemon creams. We could even venture into the silvery lavender blues that are out back, and then there are the salmons. What do you think?"

"I think you're brilliant."

"Really?"

"Really."

"And you agree? See"—she turned and delved through a sample box and brought out a crimson swatch of cloth—"we'd use a color like this only for accent."

"I agree. Wholeheartedly and unconditionally. Now can we talk about something else?"

"But we have a lot of decisions to make. Deciding on the color scheme was just the first step.

Now we have to find the prints and patterns and materials—"

He pulled her to him, angling her so that she lay across his lap. "We can do that later, can't we?"

Fire burned in the depths of his blue eyes, and her determination to discuss decorating went right out of her mind. "Absolutely," she whispered and pulled his head down so that she could capture his mouth with hers.

Nine

George Whitmark's lined face lit up in a grin when he saw Melisande climb out of her car. "Well, hello there. Haven't seen you much in the last few days."

Melisande smiled, knowing by now that he didn't mean anything by his remark, that he was just being friendly. "Yes, I know. It's been a busy time."

He nodded sagely. "People nowadays stay too busy, if you ask me. They don't have time to stop and enjoy life."

"You're absolutely right." When she first arrived here, she wouldn't have agreed with him, but this past week had opened up a world of enjoyment for her that had nothing to do with work. The days had flown by in a blur of happiness. By the third day into the week, she had stopped calling her office altogether. She hadn't been able to breathe without inhaling Cameron's scent, hadn't been able to move without him by her side, hadn't been able to sleep unless he was in bed with her. She had given in and let herself be overwhelmed by him. She had accepted, without trying to analyze, what was happening to her.

"Your stay here is almost up, isn't it?"

She had tried so hard not to think about how fast the time was passing, but here it was, her last night in Lacy. And every time she remembered that this was her last night, she wanted to cry. "Yes, it is."

"I sure do hate to see you go. It's been a pleasure having you. It's kind of nice to have company every now and then. That's the reason I'm sprucing up the place. I hope it'll bring more folks in. By the way, I took your advice"—he held up the paint stirrer so that she could see the blue paint that coated it—"four cabins are going to be blue."

"That's great. I don't think you'll be sorry. I'll come say good-bye before I leave tomorrow."

In the cabin she raised the windows, then turned on the radio and scanned the dial until she found easy-listening music. Cameron had been puzzled, but she had insisted on coming back to the motel to change for the Founders Day Dance.

She needed some time alone to catch her breath and to steel herself against their inevitable parting tomorrow. Also, she had decided that if this was to be their last night together, she wanted to look her very best.

Leaving the bathroom door open, she took a long, luxurious bath that she had scented with oil. The music, the ever-fragrant breeze, and the scented water soaked into her pores, soothing her. Much to her surprise, she had come to enjoy baths this past week, especially, she thought with a secret smile, when Cameron was in the tub with her.

When at last she climbed out, she dried off, and as always worked gel through her hair. Then, pausing to check the time, she discovered she wasn't wearing her watch. Staring at her wrist, she tried to remember where she had left her watch, or even when was the last time she had seen it. She couldn't. Another change that Cameron had wrought in her, she thought. But she had no doubt that once she was back in Dallas, her watch would once more become an indispensable part of her life.

Her heart was heavy with the thought as she set about getting ready. She pressed a light foundation onto her face, pleased that she no longer had to use concealer to try to hide the shadows beneath her eyes. They were completely gone.

She darkened her lashes and finished off her makeup with blusher and eye shadow. Then while her hair dried, she sat out on the steps and leisurely painted her toenails and fingernails a soft pink color. The whole process of spending time on herself—so unusual for her—preparing for an evening out with Cameron, restored at least part of her spirits and made her feel deliciously female. It was a time to be savored, a time to be stored up for future remembrances, a time to keep at bay the all-engulfing sadness she knew would come when she left Lacy and Cameron behind.

When she pulled the dress she planned to wear from the closet where it had been hanging for the last week, she once again silently applauded Noelle's exquisite taste. The white and gold evening frock looked like a little girl's pinafore, with its white bib front and short, full white skirt. But its resemblance to a child's dress ended there. Melisande put it on, carefully adjusting the gold ribboned straps that seductively crisscrossed her bare back three times, and the shiny, gold, ruffled petticoats that peeked out from beneath the skirt in a sexy froth, leaving a long, shapely length of her legs to show. She stepped into a pair of gold strapped heels just in time to go to the door to greet Cameron when he knocked.

His eyes darkened as he took in her appearance. "Do you honestly think I'm going to be able to let you out of the cabin without making love to you?"

She was having a similar problem with him. He was startlingly handsome in a black evening suit with a crisp white shirt and sophisticated designer tie. "You look wonderful yourself." So wonderful, she thought wryly, her carefully applied nail polish was in danger of melting right off.

"And you look like someone I don't want to let out of my sight all evening."

She smiled, delighted to her feminine core. "I decided to pull out all the stops for tonight, since the place will no doubt be packed with smooth-haired women."

He shook his head as if he couldn't believe what he was hearing. "Whoever told you smooth hair was better than curly?"

"Cameron, my hair isn't just *curly*, it's totally *fried*."

He laughed. "Whatever it is, it's my favorite kind of hair."

"You're just saying that," she murmured with a pleased grin, "but thank you anyway."

He reached for her and pulled her to him. "Would you like me to convince you that I'm not just saying it?"

She'd love it, she thought. "We don't have time." Her tone was regretful. "I've misplaced my watch, but we must be late as it is."

"We don't have to go at all, Melisande."

"I'm afraid we do. I promised Phyllis that I'd get you there. She seems to think it important that you attend, plus I think she wants us there for support. She and John have a *date* for the dance, and she's nervous." From what Phyllis had told them, faced with losing her, John had quickly gotten his Type A personality under control and had sorted through his priorities. This was a big night out for them. Phyllis had promised him she would move her things back into their house tomorrow.

Cameron grimaced, but humor glimmered in his eyes. "Don't I know it. She's acting just like she did when she was a teenager. I had to put up with it then, I don't think I should have to now."

Mischievously she poked at his chest. "Oh, and I suppose you've never been nervous about a date."

"Nervous? Yeah, I was a little nervous about tonight. I didn't like letting you come over here alone. I kept having visions of me showing up here and finding you gone."

She toyed with one of the pearl buttons on his shirt. "I probably should have stood you up, if for no other reason than to turn the tables on you for all the women I'm sure you've stood up over the years."

He growled playfully. "How many times have I got to tell you? There's only been one woman in my life—*you.*"

Just for tonight, their last night together, she decided to believe him.

"Lacy Civic Center?" Melisande read the name of the building as Cameron pulled his car into a parking space in the spacious lot. "What a nice place."

"It's new. In fact the dance tonight is the first official event to be held here."

Staring at the graceful lines of the glass-and-brick building, she suddenly wished she and Cameron were back at the house, alone, just the two of them. Tomorrow he would give her his decision about the bed, and then she would get into her car and drive back to Dallas and never see him again. She wanted, *needed* to be alone with him.

"We don't have to stay long," he said softly. "In fact we can leave right now. Just say the word."

She smiled wryly. "You did it again. You read my mind."

"No. I just said what was on *my* mind."

The man was positively incredible. She slowly exhaled, trying to regain her equilibrium. "You need to be there for Phyllis, and I'm looking forward to the dance." The last part was a lie, and before she could change her mind and beg him to take her back to the house, she opened the car door and stepped out. "Let's go."

They had barely made it inside the front doors when Elizabeth appeared in front of them, glamorous and sophisticated, dressed in a figure-hugging black sheath. With an intimate smile of welcome, she fixed her blue eyes on Cameron. "I'm so glad you were able to make it this evening. At the rate you've been turning down invitations, I was afraid you wouldn't come."

Quite deliberately he drew Melisande to his side. "You remember Melisande, don't you, Elizabeth?"

Though her smile stayed in place, it lost its welcome as she turned to Melisande. "Hello. You're still in town? I thought you said you were just passing through."

Cameron spoke before Melisande could form a

reply. "I managed to convince her to extend her stay."

"How nice . . ."

Melisande mentally sighed. Here they went again. *Nice*, as in *terrible, awful, disastrous*. If she'd been at her mental best, she supposed she would have once again reversed her decision on Elizabeth, but this time she decided it wasn't worth the effort.

Elizabeth took in Melisande's attire with an appraising eye. "What an . . . interesting dress. Tell me, Melisande, have you ever considered using lemon juice on your freckles? It wouldn't take them away completely, but it would fade them and improve your overall appearance enormously."

Then again, Melisande thought, maybe it was worth the effort after all.

Once more Cameron answered for her. "Melisande is too smart to do something as stupid as that, Elizabeth. She knows how much I love her freckles."

Elizabeth's unblemished skin lost a considerable amount of its color. "You do?"

"Every time I look at them, I get turned on." He smiled pleasantly. "Have a nice evening, Elizabeth." Still holding Melisande's hand, he led her through the foyer and into the large, mood-lit auditorium, where an orchestra played and a large crowd was already dancing.

Out on the dance floor, held in his arms, Melisande tilted her head back and looked up at him, dangerously close to laughter. "Cameron, you shouldn't have said that."

"Why not? The woman is insufferably rude. Besides, it's true." He momentarily freed his hand from hers and brushed the tips of his fingers over the sprinkling of freckles that dusted one cheek. "I have this great urge to kiss every freckle on your body."

An intoxicating weakness swept through her, and Melisande promptly forgot about Elizabeth. "Thank you."

He slipped his fingers beneath the gold straps at the back of her dress and brought his hand to rest on her bare skin. "For what?" he asked huskily, his mouth close to her ear so that she could hear him over the music. "For wanting you? For telling the truth? For not decking Elizabeth? Believe me, if she were a man, I would have."

"You shouldn't put your hand under my straps. It'll look . . ."

"Like I can't stand not having my hands on you? I *can't*."

High above the dancer's heads a mirrored ball revolved. As Melisande and Cameron moved slowly to the music, ricochets of mirrored light flashed over them. In the circle of his arms she softened, and her surroundings receded. She gazed up into the blue of his eyes and fought against the urge to let herself drown in them. "Thank you for convincing me to stay the past week. I've had a glorious time."

"Then stay the summer."

With a small smile she shook her head sadly. "Don't even start. There's just no way."

"That's what you said about a week." He pulled her more closely against him, crushing her breasts against his chest, making her aware of his obvious desire.

She breathed in, smelling his virility, his male flesh, and their mutual desire. It made her light-headed, and she fought to maintain her sanity. "I can't stay, Cameron."

"All right, then. I won't pester you about it."

No matter what she said to the contrary, she found that deep down, she wanted him to argue with her, to make promises and say outrageous things to try to keep her with him a little longer. But instead he had taken her at her word and followed her wishes.

She had been caught up in an enchanted spell this past week, living at a slower pace, eating and sleeping regularly, laughing, making love. . . . Even the prospect of getting the bed had lessened in importance. But now, she realized, she was going to have to break out of the spell somehow if she was ever going to be able to get in her car and drive away.

His fingers flexed on her back, scorching her skin. She had to stifle a moan. He didn't understand what he did to her, but she was going to incinerate right here on the dance floor in full sight of the good citizens of Lacy if she couldn't discipline her feelings. Seeking a diversion, she scanned the people around them. "I wonder where Phyllis is?"

"Don't worry about her. She'll find us."

They were near the edge of the dance floor, and she noticed a petite doll of a woman, standing with a congenial-looking group. Her attention was riveted on Cameron. "There's a woman over there who can't seem to take her eyes off you."

He maneuvered them so that he could catch a glance of the woman Melisande had indicated. "That's Mary Ann."

"The lawyer you seem to think would squeal at the sight of a mouse and who makes a pecan pie that's simply heaven?"

"The very one."

"She's extremely pretty."

"Ummm."

His fingers restlessly stroked her back, heating her blood and starting an ache between her legs. It was a condition she had grown accustomed to, a condition she loved. His actions weren't making it easy for her on any level. "You mean, you're not in the least bit interested?"

He angled his head so that he could look down at her. "How could I possibly be interested in anyone when I've got you in my arms?"

"You won't have me in your arms tomorrow night." She felt compelled to point the fact out, but she paid the price with a vague pain in her stomach.

He smiled down at her. "You're beautiful."

The pain disappeared. "I'd like to be able to tell you to stop saying things like that, but somehow I can't quite get up any conviction about it." He chuckled, and she glanced at Mary Ann again. "She's eyeing you if you were a three-course meal and she's starving."

"Don't let her size fool you. I doubt if she's ever missed a meal in her life."

"Well, her tongue is practically dragging the floor. It could even be a hazard. If she's not careful, people will trip over it."

"The only tongue I'm interested in is yours," he murmured thickly. "Give it to me."

"*Cameron.*"

He dipped his head and placed his mouth against hers. "Give it to me," he whispered, his lips moving against hers.

Heat flooded every cell of her body, and her head swam. She opened her mouth, and his tongue slipped in to find and tangle with hers. She slid her hand around his neck, through the length of his hair that lay against his collar, and clung to him. The kiss he was giving her and that she was returning had no place in a crowd, she thought helplessly. It belonged in a darkened bedroom where there was only the two of them and they could shed their clothes and follow up the kiss with the ecstasy of lovemaking that her body was already craving.

But despite their surroundings, Cameron didn't back off on the kiss. He delved his tongue deeper, kissing her with breathtaking thoroughness until she was shuddering mindlessly in his arms. Then and only then did he end the kiss. And opening her eyes, she felt as though the room was spinning around her.

He nuzzled his mouth against her ear, and his fingers rubbed against the bare flesh of her back. "Let's get out of here."

The music kept the sound of her moan from reaching the dancers close to them. She was in a hopeless situation, being drawn deeper and deeper into the spell and fast losing her resolve to escape it.

Cameron rested his forehead against hers, continuing to sway with her in time to the music. "Melisande?" He drew the hand that was holding hers inward so that it was between them. Then he slipped his fingers beneath the side edge of the pinafore top and touched the softness of her breast. "I want you, Melisande." His words were a growl of need. "Can we go?"

Why deprive herself of something she wanted so badly? It was stupid and a lost cause anyway. She wanted him every bit as badly as he wanted her. "We'll leave as soon as we see Phyllis."

"Then let's go find her and get the hell out of here." Taking her hand, he led her from the dance floor.

"Hello, Cameron."

With a silent curse he stopped. "Hello, Lisa."

Lisa. Melisande's head instantly cleared as she looked at the lovely woman standing in front of them. And her heart plummeted.

Lisa was everything Melisande could imagine that Cameron would want for his wife. She had the inevitable smooth hair of the women in Lacy, and to make matters worse, her hair was a wonderful champagne blond, the color of winter wheat that only Mother Nature could have provided. Her dress was a sparkling designer number, perfect both for the occasion and for her. And she had liquid-brown eyes that gleamed with kindness and warmth. Melisande couldn't find a thing wrong with her.

The caption beneath this woman's picture would have to be:

Cameron's Wife.

With a genuine smile Lisa held out her hand to her. "You must be Melisande. Phyllis has told me so much about you, I feel I already know you. I'm only sorry we haven't met before."

Even though Melisande was able to shake Lisa's hand, she wasn't able to talk. For the life of her she couldn't think of a word to say to the exquisite creature before her. In fact she had the strangest urge to cry.

"Lisa, have you seen Phyllis?" Cameron asked.

Lisa's smiled widened. "She and John were dancing the last time I saw them over on the other side of the room, and they looked blissfully happy."

"Thank goodness for that."

Lisa nodded in heartfelt agreement, and watching her, Melisande saw Lisa's eyes grow soft as she gazed at Cameron. Lisa was in love with Cameron.

It was an expression only another woman would recognize, another woman who felt the same way about him.

An electric shock ran straight through Melisande. Lord help her, *she* loved him too.

"There were times this past week," Lisa was saying, "that I wasn't sure what was going to happen with those two. I knew they belonged together, but Phyllis was so hurt, I didn't see how it would work out."

Holding Melisande's hand, Cameron sensed more than felt that she had stiffened. He let go of her hand and put his arm around her, drawing her close against him. "I think John needed the jolt of her leaving him to wake him up to what was happening, and she needed the time and distance away from him to see what she was about to lose." Absently rubbing his hand up and down Melisande's arm, he continued speaking with Lisa. "Thank you for letting Phyllis stay with you this past week."

"I was happy to have her."

"Normally she could have come and stayed with me, but the house is pretty torn up, and I have only one bed set up at the moment."

Shadows that only Melisande noticed came and went in Lisa's eyes, and she realized that Lisa was aware that she had been spending the nights in Cameron's bed.

"It's all right, really," Lisa said. "I understood that you were busy, and I was glad to help."

Lisa's sincerity made Melisande like and admire her all the more. Given the same set of circumstances, she wouldn't have been able to be half as gracious.

Lisa turned to Melisande. "Now that Phyllis and

John are back together, I'd love to have you over for tea."

"Thank you. That's very kind of you, but I'm leaving tomorrow to go back home."

A spark of hope flared, then died in Lisa's eyes. "I'm sorry to hear that. Maybe on your next visit we can get together."

There would be no point in telling her that she wasn't coming back, Melisande decided. Maybe once she was gone and Cameron forgot about her, he would tell Lisa.

Lisa glanced over Cameron's shoulder, then smiled up at him. "Phyllis and John are headed this way. I'll let the four of you talk." Her smile remained as she turned to Melisande. "Good-bye. Please come back and see us soon."

"'Bye, Lisa. It was lovely meeting you." And she meant it.

Cameron frowned down at Melisande. "Are you all right?"

"Fine." She had never been more miserable in her life. She had just simultaneously discovered that she was in love with him and had met the perfect woman for him. She already knew all the reasons why her love for Cameron wouldn't work out, and to add to her agony, she could see it was only a matter of time before he realized he should spend the rest of his life with Lisa.

"Well, hello, you two," Cameron said as Phyllis and her husband walked up. "You certainly look as if you're having a good time."

"We are," Phyllis said, radiant in her happiness. "Melisande, that is a breathtaking dress. You look fabulous."

She barely heard her. "Thank you," she replied automatically.

The good-looking man at Phyllis's side grinned

and extended his hand to Melisande. "Phyllis told me you were beautiful."

"She did?" she said, numbly taking his hand. She felt as if she were in a fog, yet at the same time she could see everything around her in sharp, excruciatingly bright focus.

"She sure did, and she didn't exaggerate. She also told me some of the things you said to her about us. I can't thank you enough."

She wished Cameron would quit running his hands up and down her arms. His touch was causing her pain. *Breathing* was causing her pain. "No thanks are necessary. I'm just glad you two have gotten back together."

John nodded. "I'm afraid I lost sight of what's important and forgot why I was working so hard in the first place." He hugged Phyllis. "*She* was the reason. I guess I was trying to live up to her brother and make her proud of me."

Phyllis placed a loving hand on John's chest. "What he didn't realize was that I was proud of him all along."

Feeling as though she had just missed something very important, Melisande looked from one to the other. "Live up to her brother?"

Just then the orchestra stopped playing, a drumroll reverberated out over the room, and a tall, silver-haired man stepped up to the microphone.

"Good evening, ladies and gentlemen. Isn't it great to see everyone having such a good time?"

The crowd broke into applause, and Cameron leaned down and whispered in her ear. "That's the mayor."

Melisande didn't care who it was. She felt as if her heart was about to break into a thousand pieces, and all she could think about was getting out of the building and away from Cameron. But he still held her against him, and the mayor continued speaking.

"This is the date of our annual Founders Day Dance, but tonight we also have something else very special to celebrate, the opening of the new Lacy Civic Center." He paused while the crowd applauded again, and then he continued. "So many people have worked hard to make this night come to pass, and they're all listed in your program. But tonight I want to single out one very extraordinary Lacy son and let you all thank him. Cameron Tate, are you here?"

Melisande heard Cameron curse beneath his breath, then John slapped Cameron on the back. "Here he is," he called out happily.

The mayor spotted them and waved his hand. "Cameron, come on up here."

Cameron leaned toward her. "Stay right here. I promise this will be as short as I can make it, and as soon as I get back, we'll leave. John, make sure she doesn't move."

"Sure thing. Melisande, you heard him. You're in our custody until he gets back."

Phyllis smiled at her.

"I don't understand," Melisande murmured, but no one heard her, because the crowd was applauding as Cameron made his way up onto the stage.

The mayor was speaking again. "This civic center was an ambitious undertaking for a town the size of Lacy, but we went for it because we felt it would benefit all of us and give our kids a place to go for their activities. And because of this man's personal check for one million dollars, our civic center is debt-free tonight. Cameron . . ."

Melisande saw Cameron step up to the microphone, but she didn't hear his remarks. She was too busy trying to assimilate the fact that Cameron had given the city a check for one million dollars.

She wasn't aware of time passing, but Cameron was suddenly at her side, his hand on her elbow, saying good-bye to those around him as he guided her out of the building.

"Thank goodness that's over," he muttered once they were outside. "I was hoping to avoid that little scene. Let's go home."

"I want to go back to the motel," she said.

He glanced curiously down at her. "Why?"

She lied. "There's something I need to do there."

"All right. But promise me you'll hurry with whatever it is. If I don't get you all to myself soon, I'm not going to be accountable for the consequences."

Ten

Cameron pulled his big car in front of Cabin 6 and turned the ignition off. "Are you going to be long?"

She turned to him. "Before I go in, I have a question."

Shifting, he angled his big body crosswise against the door and the seat and looked at her. During the drive to the motel she had spoken only in monosyllables. "What?"

"What it is that you do for a living? And don't say only things that you love."

He smiled, relieved that his occupation was the only thing bothering her. He had been afraid that someone or something had upset her back at the dance. "But it's the truth."

"Yeah, okay, but what *exactly* do you do that you love to make you enough money that you can afford to give the city a million dollars?"

He made a casual gesture with his hand. "I'm the founder and CEO of the Mesa chain."

Her mouth dropped open. The Mesa was an extremely large chain of highly successful Southwestern restaurants. "You're *that* C. R. Tate?"

"Cameron Robert Tate, at your service."

"But what are you doing here, restoring a house?"

He reached out and closed a hand in her hair. "Pretty much what I've already told you. I grew up in this town, I always admired the house, my sister was going through a bad time, so I decided to take time off, be with her, and have a little fun with the house."

"Your headquarters are in Dallas," she murmured. He had said he might use the house as a second home, and it hadn't occurred to her to ask where his first home was.

"That's right. In fact, living in Dallas was my ace in the hole. If you hadn't agreed to stay, I would have followed you back to Dallas."

"You would have pursued me?"

"What do you think?"

She wasn't sure. Her mind was going ten different ways. And then suddenly she started to laugh, a laugh more ironic than humorous.

He tugged on a coiled ginger curl. "What's so funny?"

"It just occurred to me that this past week might not have happened if I had known who you are that night I walked into your house."

"Why?"

"Knowing who you are is the *one* thing in the world that would have taken my mind off the bed. The Mesa would be a spectacular account for my company to acquire, and believe me, I've tried everything for a chance to pitch ideas to you, but you and your people are absolutely unapproachable. If I had known who you are, I would have seen it as a golden opportunity."

He was silent for a moment. "You realize, don't you, that I could have told you who I was right at the beginning, that I could have used Mesa as a means to keep you with me?"

"Why didn't you?"

"I wanted you to come to know me for myself and not for what my business could do for you."

"But I still wanted something from you. The bed."

"It's not the same thing."

She laughed again, the same humorless laugh. "I guess you're right. At that point I would have said to hell with my insomnia and gone after your account."

"The account is yours."

Her mouth dropped open again, but this time her recovery was quicker. "No, Cameron. I don't want your company's account." Hearing herself, she stopped, shocked. But it was true. During the past week her priorities had shifted, and she had discovered there were other things more important to her than business.

"Why not?" he asked.

Because she loved him. Because after spending a week of deep, absorbing, engrossing intimacy with him, she wouldn't be able to stand having only a business relationship with him. "Because when I win an account, I like to know its because of my ideas and not because I went to bed with the boss."

"Melisande," he said, his tone gently chiding, "I already know your ideas are going to be good. I've had a week's exposure to that quick brain of yours. There's not a doubt in my mind that you'll do a beautiful job for my company."

She shook her head. "It can't happen. A business relationship would be impossible after the week we just spent."

"I disagree."

His meaning sank in, and her eyes slowly widened in shock. "You can't think that we're going to see each other after tomorrow!"

"Yes, Melisande, I do."

She couldn't let it happen. She loved him, and that meant she couldn't abide having less than everything of him. "I came here to acquire a bed, not a lover."

"You can have the damn bed. Now, what's wrong with being lovers? I don't remember hearing any complaints this past week."

"You can't give me the bed because you think we're going to continue seeing each other in Dallas. We're not."

"I've already told you that one has nothing to do with the other. The bed is yours. Okay? No strings. You can *have* the bed. Now, let's talk about us. Why is everything going to be different once we go back to Dallas?"

He might think she had a quick mind, but at the moment his was far quicker. She felt like a wounded animal who wanted nothing more than to go someplace dark and quiet where it could lick its wounds. "I'm going in now. I've decided to spend the night here."

"Why?"

She nervously plucked at the hem of her dress. "I want to be alone tonight. I'll be over in the morning to find out what your decision is regarding the bed."

"I've already told you my decision. It's yours."

She shook her head, but at what she didn't know. She just knew that she couldn't take one more second of being in the close confines of his car with him. She opened the door and bolted for the cabin.

Cameron walked into the cabin behind her and slammed shut the door. "This conversation isn't over."

Feeling cornered, she whirled to face him. "Cameron, please leave."

"Not until we've settled a few things, starting with why you want to be alone now that we're here, when with one more kiss I could have made love to you on the dance floor."

She fought back tears. She wanted him so much, she was shaking with it, but she couldn't make love to him without revealing the secret of her heart. And above everything else, she had to at least try to leave Lacy with her pride and her dignity intact. "Maybe I'm tired of spending every night with you, have you thought of that?"

"Try again, Melisande." He shrugged out of his jacket and tossed it on a chair.

"Don't get too comfortable. You're about to leave."

Deliberately tugging on his tie and loosening it, he turned the full force of his hard gaze on her. "I'm not going anywhere, not until you level with me."

Anger flared up in her until she was nearly choking with it. "What's the matter, Cameron? You've got at *least* three women back at the civic center who would love to spend the night with you. Isn't that enough? All you have to do is go back over there and take your pick. But think twice about Elizabeth. The more I see her, the more bovine she seems to become."

"You're the *only* woman I'm interested in."

Her nerves felt like live electrical wires, arcing and zapping. "Sure. Right now. Tonight. But tomorrow when I leave, the other women will be waiting to fill your bed. Which one are you going to choose? Elizabeth, Mary Ann, or Lisa? Or maybe one of the others I haven't met?"

"Are you through?"

"I haven't even begun. The minute I laid eyes on you, I knew you'd be able to sell anything to anyone. What I didn't realize was that I was up against a man notorious for making cutthroat deals, and I didn't have a chance. I bought staying the week. Isn't that enough?"

"Not by a long shot."

"Tough. It's going to have to be. The fact is, I don't want to spend the night with you. It's as simple as that."

"I don't believe you. What's happened, Melisande? Was it something at the dance? What was it?"

Her hands clenched into fists at her side. "Do you have that big of an ego? Can't you accept that I might be tired of you?"

"With one kiss I could have you begging for me."

"*Bastard*."

"Maybe. Probably. Shall we test it out?" He took a step toward her.

Her hand came up like a shield. "*No*. Stay away from me!"

"Not a chance in hell."

A shudder racked through her body, and she turned away. Silence pulsated loudly between them, hammering against her eardrums.

"Melisande?" His unexpectedly soft voice sliced through the loud silence and touched her hurting heart.

She didn't answer him for fear something in her tone would give away her pain. She wrapped her arms around herself, seeking comfort—but found none.

"I don't want you to feel that I will threaten your career. As long as it makes you happy, I'll be happy. My career is still important to me. It's just that I've learned to trust the people I've hired to take some of the burden off me. Hopefully you'll learn to do the same thing. But even if you don't, it doesn't matter. It's obvious you love what you do, and I would never get in the way of your success. Believe it, because it's the truth."

Bewildered, she slowly turned to face him. "Get in the way of my success? What are you talking about?"

"I love you, Melisande. I want you to marry me. I want you to be my wife."

She went cold, then hot, then cold again. It seemed to her as if the room expanded, then contracted, and at the same time all the lights in the cabin dimmed.

"Don't be afraid, Melisande."

Afraid? Was that what was wrong with her? She should be happy. He had just told her that he loved her, and heaven knew she loved him. But, yes, she thought, she was scared out of her mind. "I don't even know where my *watch* is," she said, her voice accusing and shrill. "It's disappeared. What have you done with it? Where is it?"

"It's back at the house on the nightstand. Okay?"

Tears sprang into her eyes. She stared numbly at him.

"I know you don't think a loving, lasting relationship is possible for you," he said gently, "but you're wrong. It is."

She didn't see him move, but suddenly he was in front of her and his hands were clasped on her upper arms.

"I know you don't love me yet, but for now my

love for you is enough. It's the base we're going to build the rest of our lives on."

"Cameron—" Amazement finally pierced her paralyzed mind. "You love me?"

"If you'd driven out of here any time this past week, I would have been right behind you."

"But what about the house, the renovation?"

"Phyllis and John are happy again. I could close up the house and leave the rest of the work until the next time I come. Or I can hire someone to supervise the work in my absence. I have detailed plans, plus you've written out your decorating ideas. There are *alternatives*, Melisande. Life can be adapted when you find something better than you've ever had before, and that's what I've found in you. What's really important is not the house, it's *you*. I can't imagine getting through a day without seeing you or a night without holding you."

The tears spilled down her cheeks. "I know," she whispered, trembling. "I've been wondering how I was going to be able to function without you once I got back to Dallas."

His hands tightened on her arms. "Does that mean you love me?"

Her throat hurt with suppressed emotion. She tried to swallow, but couldn't. "I love you, but . . ."

He smiled, triumphantly, tenderly. "I know— you're afraid. But, Melisande, trust me. You're going to be able to have everything you want. I have you, and we're going to spend the rest of our lives together."

She brought a hand up to brush away her tears. Once again reason and logic didn't have a place. All of her carefully laid plans seemed insignificant. He said she could have everything, and she believed him without qualification. "All I want, all I'll *ever* want, is you."

With a husky laugh, he drew her to him and kissed her slowly and deeply until they were both weak and quivering, and then he took her to bed.

The morning light filtered softly through the cabin windows, along with the perfumed air of Lacy. Melisande stretched, her naked body arching, supple and lazy as a cat. Cameron's warm, strong body was sprawled beside her, his arm across her waist, watching her.

She subsided back beside him. "You know what I just realized? I just slept through the night, and I did it on a bed that wasn't Aunt Sarah's!"

He came up on an elbow and gazed down at her, his intense blue eyes twinkling with love and humor. "I've been meaning to tell you something."

She stroked a finger along his beard-shadowed jaw. "Oh, yeah? What's that?"

"The reason you were able to sleep through the night at my house was not because of your Aunt Sarah's bed."

A brief frown came and went on her face. "Of course it was."

"No, it couldn't have been. You see, you weren't sleeping on your Aunt Sarah's mattress. The mattress you've been sleeping on at the house is not the same mattress you slept on when you were a child. Remember when I told you I had gotten new linens?"

"Yes."

"Well, at the same time I also had a new mattress made to replace the original."

A *new* mattress.

She slowly smiled as realization dawned.

She had slept, not because of a bed but because of him and the deep, all-encompassing happiness she had felt being with him, even if at first it had been unconscious.

"I love you," he said quietly.

"I love you," she answered.

And she held out her arms and he went into them.

THE EDITOR'S CORNER

What could be more romantic than Valentine's Day and six LOVESWEPT romances all in one glorious month! Celebrate this special time of the year by cuddling up with the wonderful books coming your way soon.

The first of our reading treasures is **ANGELS SINGING** by Joan Elliott Pickart, LOVESWEPT #594. Drew Sloan's first impression of Memory Lawson isn't the best, considering she's pointing a shotgun at him and accusing him of trespassing on her mountain. But the heat that flashes between them convinces him to stay and storm the walls around her heart . . . until she believes that she's just the kind of warm, loving woman he's been looking for. Joan comes through once more with a winning romance!

We have a real treat in store for fans of Kay Hooper. After a short hiatus for work on **THE DELANEY CHRISTMAS CAROL** and other books, Kay returns with **THE TOUCH OF MAX,** LOVESWEPT #595, the *fiftieth* book in her illustrious career! If you were a fan of Kay's popular "Hagan Strikes Again" and "Once Upon a Time" series, you'll be happy to know that **THE TOUCH OF MAX** is the first of four "Men of Mysteries Past" books, all of which center around Max Bannister's priceless gem collection, which the police are using as bait to catch a notorious thief. But when innocent Dinah Layton gets tangled in the trap, it'll take that special touch of Max to set her free . . . and capture her heart. A sheer delight—and it'll have you breathlessly waiting for more. Welcome back, Kay!

In Charlotte Hughes's latest novel, Crescent City's new soccer coach is **THE INCREDIBLE HUNK,** LOVE-SWEPT #596. Utterly male, gorgeously virile, Jason Profitt has the magic touch with kids. What more perfect guy could there be for a redhead with five children to raise! But Maggie Farnsworth is sure that once he's seen her chaotic life, he'll run for the hills. Jason has another plan of action in mind, though—to make a home in her loving arms. Charlotte skillfully blends humor and passion in this page-turner of a book.

Appropriately enough, Marcia Evanick's contribution to the month, **OVER THE RAINBOW,** LOVESWEPT #597, is set in a small town called Oz, where neither Hillary Walker nor Mitch Ferguson suspects his kids of matchmaking when he's forced to meet the lovely speech teacher. The plan works so well the kids are sure they'll get a mom for Christmas. But Hillary has learned never to trust her heart again, and only Mitch's passionate persuasion can change her mind. You can count on Marcia to deliver a fun-filled romance.

A globetrotter in buckskins and a beard, Nick Leclerc has never considered himself **THE FOREVER MAN,** LOVESWEPT #598, by Joan J. Domning. Yet when he appears in Carla Hudson's salon for a haircut and a shave, her touch sets his body on fire and fills him with unquenchable longing. The sexy filmmaker has leased Carla's ranch to uncover an ancient secret, but instead he finds newly awakened dreams of hearth and home. Joan will capture your heart with this wonderful love story.

Erica Spindler finishes this dazzling month with **TEMPT-ING CHANCE,** LOVESWEPT #599. Shy Beth Waters doesn't think she has what it takes to light the sensual spark in gorgeous Chance Michaels. But the outrageous results of her throwing away a chain letter finally convince her that she's woman enough to tempt Chance— and that he's more than eager to be caught in her embrace. Humorous, yet seething with emotion and desire, **TEMPTING CHANCE** is one tempting morsel from talented Erica.

Look for four spectacular novels on sale now from FANFARE. Award-winning Iris Johansen confirms her place as a major star with **THE TIGER PRINCE,** a magnificent new historical romance that sweeps from exotic realms to the Scottish highlands. In a locked room of shadows and sandalwood, Jane Barnaby meets adventurer Ruel McClaren and is instantly transformed from a hard-headed businesswoman to the slave of a passion she knows she must resist.

Suzanne Robinson first introduced us to Blade in **LADY GALLANT,** and now in the new thrilling historical romance **LADY DEFIANT,** Blade returns as a bold, dashing hero. One of Queen Elizabeth's most dangerous spies, he must romance a beauty named Oriel who holds a clue that could change history. Desire builds and sparks fly as these two unwillingly join forces to thwart a deadly conspiracy.

Hailed by Katherine Stone as "emotional, compelling, and triumphant!", **PRIVATE SCANDALS** is the debut novel by very talented Christy Cohen. From the glamour of New York to the glitter of Hollywood comes a heartfelt story of scandalous desires and long-held secrets . . . of dreams realized and longings denied . . . of three remarkable women whose lifelong friendship would be threatened by one man.

Available once again is **A LOVE FOR ALL TIME** by bestselling author Dorothy Garlock. In this moving tale, Casey Farrow gives up all hope of a normal life when a car crash leaves indelible marks on her breathtaking beauty . . . until Dan Farrow, the man who rescued her from the burning vehicle, convinces her that he loves her just the way she is.

Also on sale this month in the hardcover edition from Doubleday is **THE LADY AND THE CHAMP** by Fran Baker. When a former Golden Gloves champion meets an elegant, uptown girl, the result is a stirring novel of courageous love that Julie Garwood has hailed as "unforgettable."

Happy reading!

With warmest wishes,

Nita Taublib

Nita Taublib
Associate Publisher
LOVESWEPT and FANFARE

THE TIGER PRINCE

by Iris Johansen
the nationally bestselling author of
THE GOLDEN BARBARIAN

From the shimmering cities of a faraway land to the heather-scented hills of the Scottish Highlands comes this passionate tale of adventure and dangerous desire by one of America's bestselling and beloved authors.

In a locked room of shadows and sandalwood, Jane Barnaby first met the wickedly disturbing man whose searing blue eyes and brazen smile seemed to read her deepest desires—a man who exuded the mystery and danger of exotic lands. In his mesmerizing presence, Jane found herself instantly transformed from a hardheaded businesswoman to the willing slave of a passion she knew she must resist.

In the following scene from the opening pages of the novel, we see how a young Jane Barnaby tries to escape the poverty of the American west to begin her world-spanning adventure . . . .

Promontory Point, Utah
November 25, 1869

"Wait!"

Dear God, he hadn't heard her. He was still striding across the wooden platform toward the train. In a moment he would be out of reach.

Panic soared through Jane Barnaby and she broke into a run, the faded skirts of her calico gown ballooning behind her. Ignoring the pain caused by the ice shards piercing her feet through the holes in the thin soles of her boots, she tore through ice-coated mud puddles down the wheel-rutted street toward the platform over a hundred yards away. "Please! Don't go!"

Patrick Reilly's expression was only a blur in the post-dawn grayness, but he must have heard her call, for he hesitated for an instant before continuing toward the train, his long legs quickly covering the distance between the station house and the passenger railway car.

He was leaving her.

Fear caught in her throat, and she desperately tried to put on more speed. The train was already vibrating, puffing, flexing its metal muscles as it prepared to spring forward down the track. "Wait for me!"

He kept his face turned straight ahead, ignoring her.

Anger, fired by desperation, flared within her and she bellowed, "Dammit, do you hear me? Don't you *dare* get on that train!"

He stopped in midstride, his big shoulders braced militantly beneath the gray-checked coarse wool of his coat. He turned with a frown to watch her dashing toward him down the platform.

She skidded to a stop before him. "I'm goin' with you."

"The hell you are. I told you last night at Frenchie's you were to stay here."

"You gotta take me."

"I don't have to do nothin'." He scowled down at her. "Go back to your ma. She'll be looking for you."

"No, she won't." She took a step closer to him. "You know all she cares about is her pipe. She don't care where I am. She won't mind if I go with you."

He shook his head.

"You know it's true." Jane moistened her lips. "I'm goin' with you. She doesn't want me. She never wanted me."

"Well, I don't want you to eith—" A flush deepened his already ruddy cheeks, and his Irish brogue thickened as he said awkwardly, "No offense, but I don't have no use for a kid in my life."

"I'm not so little, I'm almost twelve." It was only a small lie; she had just turned eleven, but he probably wouldn't remember that. She took another step closer. "You gotta take me. I belong to you."

"How many times do I have to tell you? I'm not your father."

"My mother said it was most likely you." She touched a strand of the curly red hair flopping about her thin face. "Our hair is the same, and you visited her a lot before she went on the pipe."

"So did half the men of the Union Pacific." His expression softened as he suddenly knelt in front of her. "Lots of Irishmen have red hair, Jane. Hell, I can name four men on my own crew who used to be Pearl's regulars. Why not pick on one of them?"

Because she desperately wanted it to be him. He was kinder to her than any of the other men who paid her mother for her body. Patrick Reilly was drunk more than he was sober when he came to Frenchie's tent, but he never hurt the women like some men did and even treated Jane with a rough affection whenever he saw her around. "It's you." Her jaw set stubbornly. "You can't know for certain it's not you."

His jaw set with equal obstinance. "And you don't know for certain it is me. So why don't you go back to Frenchie's and leave me alone? Christ, I wouldn't even know how to take care of you."

"Take care of me?" She stared at him in bewilderment. "Why should you do that? I take care of myself."

For an instant a flicker of compassion crossed his craggy features. "I guess you've had to do enough of that all right. With your ma sucking on that damn opium pipe and growing up in that pimp's hovel."

She immediately pounced on the hint of softening. "I won't be a bother to you. I don't eat much and I'll stay out of your way." He was beginning to frown again, and she went on hurriedly. "Except when you have something for me to do, of course. I'm a hard worker. Ask anyone at Frenchie's. I empty slops and help in the kitchen. I sweep and mop and run errands. I can count and take care of money. Frenchie even has me time the customers on Saturday night and tell them when they've had their money's worth." She grasped his arm. "I promise I'll do anything you want me to do. Just take me with you."

"Hell, you don't under—" He was silent a moment, gazing at her pleading face before muttering, "Look, I'm a railroad man. It's all I know and my job here is over now that the tracks have been joined. I've got an offer to boss my own crew in Salisbury and that's a big chance for an ignorant mick like me. Salisbury's way across the ocean in England. You don't want to go that far away."

"Yes, I do. I don't care where we go." Her small hand tightened on his arm. "Try me. I promise you won't be sorry."

"The devil I won't be sorry." His tone was suddenly impatient as he shook off her grasp and rose to his feet. "I won't be saddled with no whore's kid for the rest of my life. Go back to Frenchie's." He started toward the train again.

The rejection frightened but didn't surprise her. She had been rejected all her life by everyone but the inhabitants of Frenchie's crib and had learned long ago she wasn't like the children of the respectable wives who followed the railroad crews from town to town. They belonged in a world of clean crisp gowns, Saturday night baths, and church on Sunday mornings while she . . .

Jane felt suddenly sick as memories flooded back to her of the lantern-lit haze of Frenchie's tent, where the cots were separated only by dirty blankets hung on sagging ropes, the sweetish smell of the opium her mother smoked from the funny-looking glass bowl by her cot, Frenchie's hard palm striking her cheek when she wasn't quick enough to do his bidding.

She *couldn't* go back to that now that escape was so near.

Her nails dug into her palms as her hands clenched into fists at her sides. "It will do you no good to leave me. I'll only follow you."

He reached the train and placed his left foot on the metal step.

"I *will*. You belong to me."

"The hell I do."

"I'll follow you to this Saddlebury and—"

"Salisbury, and you'd have to swim the goddamn ocean."

"I'll do it. I'll find a way. You'll see that I'll find a way to—" Her voice broke and she had to stop.

"Dammit." His head lowered, his gaze fixed on the ridged metal of the step. "Why the hell do you have to be so damned stubborn?"

"Take me," she whispered. She did not know what else to say, what to offer him. "Please. If I stay, I'm scared someday I'll be like her. I . . . don't like it there."

He stood there, his shoulders hunched as moment after moment passed. "Oh, what the hell!" He whirled, jumped back down on the platform. His big, freckled hands grasped her waist and he effortlessly picked her up and lifted her onto the train. "Jesus, you're tiny. You don't weigh anything at all."

Had he given in? She was afraid to believe it. "That doesn't matter. I'm small for my age, but I'm very strong."

"You'd better be. I guess you can trail along, but it don't mean anything. I'm not your father and you'll call me Patrick like anybody else."

LADY DEFIANT
by Suzanne Robinson

Author of LADY GALLANT and
LADY HELLFIRE

"An author with star quality . . . spectacularly talented."
—*Romantic Times*

As the queen's most cunning spy, Blade Fitzstephen knew where his duty lay. Sent to romance Oriel Richmond into revealing a dangerous secret the lovely innocent did not even know she possessed, he was prepared to go to any lengths to captivate her. Oriel knew that her many lovelorn suitors were more taken with her fortune than with her beauty. Yet when she overheard the only man who had ever stirred her interest—the dark and roguish Blade—describe her in highly unflattering terms, she was more than hurt, she was furious. Never again would she harbor dreams of love . . . until the day Blade returned to Richmond Hall to press his suit, and Oriel found herself responding against all reason. . . .

If you loved LADY GALLANT, don't miss Blade's own sensuous, romantic story in LADY DEFIANT.

"May God damn you to the eternal fires," Blade said.

Oriel had been about to push the door open, but paused as she heard the young man speak. The father said nothing. His mouth was full and he chewed calmly.

"This is the fourth girl you've dragged me to see, and the worst. She's also the last."

"Clean her up and she'll be worth looking over. Jesu Maria, did you see that wild hair? Almost black, but with so much red to it there must be a spirit of fire in her to match."

"I care not. Did you think to buy my return to your side with a virgin sacrifice?"

"It's your duty to stay by my side and produce heirs."

"God's breath!" Blade took several steps toward his father, then halted and cursed again as he tried to strangle the hilt of his sword with one hand. "I won't do it. I won't marry her. She has eyes like dried peas and a pointy little face like a weasel, and she can't even remember my name."

"It's Blade." Oriel pushed the door back and stepped into the great chamber.

It had taken all her courage not to run away. His disdain had been so unexpected. He'd said those words so quickly she hadn't understood their meaning immediately, and then she realized that while she had been enraptured, he had been offended by her and her appearance. All the years of encountering youths and men who paid her slight notice came thundering back into her memory. The evenings spent watching while others danced, the hunts spent pursuing a deer or fowl while other girls were instead pursued themselves—these had driven her to seek comfort in learning and solitary pursuits.

Until today she'd scorned to seek the favor of men, for there lay the path to great hurt. She had forgotten herself and her fear this once, for the prize entranced her without warning, danced before her in the guise of a dark-haired lord with eyes like the silver edge of a cloud when lit by the sun behind it. She had forgotten, and now she paid the price.

When she'd spoken, both men had frozen. Neither had spoken as she entered, and now Blade approached her. Oriel held up a hand to stop him, and he hesitated.

"If it please you, my lord, let there be no pretense between us." Oriel stopped and swallowed, for her voice trembled. "I see that you like not my person and have no time or desire to make yourself familiar with my character. Likewise, I find myself unable to countenance a suitor with so ungentle a manner, be he ever so handsome and endowed with a goodly estate."

"Mistress, my hot and heady language was the result of being near my lord father."

"Whatever the cause, I have no wish to deal with you further. Good day to you, my lords."

Oriel turned her back on Blade and made herself walk slowly out of the great chamber, down the gallery to the staircase. She lifted her skirts and was about to dash upstairs in a race to beat the fall of her tears when she heard Blade's voice calling to her.

He was at her side before she could retreat. His cloak swirled around her skirts, and his dark form blocked out the light from the gallery windows. She could smell the leather of his riding clothes. He put a hand on her arm, and she sprang away, shaking it off.

"Mistress, stay you a moment."

"I have work, my lord." She must gain her chamber before she betrayed herself with tears.

"I swear to you, my words were hastily spoken and ill-reasoned on account of my anger at my father. A meanness of spirit overcomes me when I'm in his company for long, and this time I struck out at him and hit you instead. I take an oath before God that none of my insults are true."

"Ofttimes we speak our truest feelings when our words are least guarded, my lord."

She brushed past him and mounted the stairs with as much dignity as she could summon. Halfway up he was still looking at her from below.

"Lady, I go to France soon, and would not leave this kingdom without your forgiveness."

Oriel looked down at Blade. Even from this height he appeared as tall as a crusader tower and as beautiful as a thunderstorm in July. In a brief span she had been enthralled and rejected, and if she didn't get away from him she would throw herself on the floor and weep for what she had lost almost before she knew she wanted it.

"Of course. As a good Christian I can hardly withhold my forgiveness, and you have it. It seems to be the only thing in Richmond Hall you want. Once again, good day to you, my lord."

PRIVATE SCANDALS
by Christy Cohen

From the glamour of New York to the glitter of Hollywood, PRIVATE SCANDALS is a heartfelt story of scandalous desires and long-held secrets . . . of dreams realized and longings denied . . . of three remarkable women whose lifelong friendship would be threatened by one man.

She stood rigid as steel, her eyes cast downward, and Jackson felt a familiar sickly dread gnaw at his gut. She must have changed her mind, and this time there would be no second chances for him.

When the minister asked her to repeat her vows, she raised her head. Her gaze met his, and a warm flood of relief washed over Jackson. Her eyes, so clear and beautiful, were sure and strong and loving. She spoke her promises firmly, confidently, with the smooth voice he'd come to love as he loved no other. And when they sealed their marriage with a kiss, her lips were soft and trusting, and he could sense the smile that tugged at their corners.

In the receiving line she stood beside him, his wife, with the satin sleeve of her dress brushing against his arm. Her expression was bright and happy as she greeted their guests. He put his arm around her waist and marveled again at the way her body conformed to his so perfectly, filling in every crevice.

The guests filtered past, a blur of puckered lips and embracing arms. Jackson paid little attention. How could he when he had the woman of his dreams beside him? She brought him so much happiness, blanketed every aspect of his life with the gauze of perfection, that he often found the past forgotten, left behind like a child's blanket no longer needed for comfort. This woman gave him everything.

He was thinking of that, of the laughter that grew more frequent between them every day, of the house in New Hampshire that awaited them, when he felt her squeeze his hand. Turning quickly, he saw the color drain from her face. He followed her desperate gaze and held himself steady against a wave of dizziness when he saw what she was looking at.

"She's here," his wife said needlessly, her silky voice marred by an uncharacteristic tremor. "I can't believe she's here."

He pulled her close to him and pressed his lips to her ear. "I love you."

She stood motionless for a moment, then he watched her transform. She pulled her scared, hunched body up straight again and smiled the smile that haunted men the world over. Her eyes met his, and he saw the tears filling them.

"And I you," she said, running her fingers along his cheek.

He returned his attention to the guests and watched, out of the corner of his eye, as she approached. He couldn't help being surprised by her beauty. It had been more than three years since he'd seen her, and she seemed to have grown softer, more feminine, more fragile. She was next in line to greet them, and the guilty pangs, long banished to the unnoticed, unwanted recesses of his mind, returned with violent intensity.

Finally, she stood before them, her chin up, her fists clenched. The woman he'd left behind. The woman once cherished as his wife's best friend. The woman who had loved him so much he couldn't breathe. She stood before them after years of bitter silence and, following a deep, drawn-out sigh, began to speak.

A LOVE FOR ALL TIME
by Dorothy Garlock

"[Dorothy Garlock] gets to the real heart and soul of her characters."
—*Romantic Times*

From award-winning author Dorothy Garlock comes one of her most beloved classic romances—a beautiful, moving story of love and beauty.

When she'd first woken up in the hospital, frightened and in pain, only the gentle, masculine voice of a stranger had the power to soothe Casey Farrow. Dan Murdock had dragged her from the wreckage of her car and saved her life. He'd held her hand and lent her his strength. But now, as she contemplated a future forever altered by the scars that marred her body and ended her career, Casey wondered why Dan was still there. . . .

She didn't want his pity. She didn't need his help. And when he told her that he loved her, Casey thought he'd lost his mind. One look in the mirror was enough to convince her that no man as attractive as Dan Murdock could possibly want her . . . until the night he showed her how wrong she could be. But wanting and loving are two very different things, and now Casey wonders if theirs is truly a love that can last for all time. . . .

Don't miss this classic Dorothy Garlock romance, available for the first time in many years.

OFFICIAL RULES TO WINNERS CLASSIC SWEEPSTAKES

No Purchase necessary. To enter the sweepstakes follow instructions found elsewhere in this offer. You can also enter the sweepstakes by hand printing your name, address, city, state and zip code on a 3" x 5" piece of paper and mailing it to: Winners Classic Sweepstakes, P.O. Box 785, Gibbstown, NJ 08027. Mail each entry separately. Sweepstakes begins 12/1/91. Entries must be received by 6/1/93. Some presentations of this sweepstakes may feature a deadline for the Early Bird prize. If the offer you receive does, then to be eligible for the Early Bird prize your entry must be received according to the Early Bird date specified. Not responsible for lost, late, damaged, misdirected, illegible or postage due mail. Mechanically reproduced entries are not eligible. All entries become property of the sponsor and will not be returned.

Prize Selection/Validations: Winners will be selected in random drawings on or about 7/30/93, by VENTURA ASSOCIATES, INC., an independent judging organization whose decisions are final. Odds of winning are determined by total number of entries received. Circulation of this sweepstakes is estimated not to exceed 200 million. Entrants need not be present to win. All prizes are guaranteed to be awarded and delivered to winners. Winners will be notified by mail and may be required to complete an affidavit of eligibility and release of liability which must be returned within 14 days of date of notification or alternate winners will be selected. Any guest of a trip winner will also be required to execute a release of liability. Any prize notification letter or any prize returned to a participating sponsor, Bantam Doubleday Dell Publishing Group, Inc., its participating divisions or subsidiaries, or VENTURA ASSOCIATES, INC. as undeliverable will be awarded to an alternate winner. Prizes are not transferable. No multiple prize winners except as may be necessary due to unavailability, in which case a prize of equal or greater value will be awarded. Prizes will be awarded approximately 90 days after the drawing. All taxes, automobile license and registration fees, if applicable, are the sole responsibility of the winners. Entry constitutes permission (except where prohibited) to use winners' names and likenesses for publicity purposes without further or other compensation.

Participation: This sweepstakes is open to residents of the United States and Canada, except for the province of Quebec. This sweepstakes is sponsored by Bantam Doubleday Dell Publishing Group, Inc. (BDD), 666 Fifth Avenue, New York, NY 10103. Versions of this sweepstakes with different graphics will be offered in conjunction with various solicitations or promotions by different subsidiaries and divisions of BDD. Employees and their families of BDD, its division, subsidiaries, advertising agencies, and VENTURA ASSOCIATES, INC., are not eligible.

Canadian residents, in order to win, must first correctly answer a time limited arithmetical skill testing question. Void in Quebec and wherever prohibited or restricted by law. Subject to all federal, state, local and provincial laws and regulations.

Prizes: The following values for prizes are determined by the manufacturers' suggested retail prices or by what these items are currently known to be selling for at the time this offer was published. Approximate retail values include handling and delivery of prizes. Estimated maximum retail value of prizes: 1 Grand Prize ($27,500 if merchandise or $25,000 Cash); 1 First Prize ($3,000); 5 Second Prizes ($400 each); 35 Third Prizes ($100 each); 1,000 Fourth Prizes ($9.00 each); 1 Early Bird Prize ($5,000); Total approximate maximum retail value is $50,000. Winners will have the option of selecting any prize offered at level won. Automobile winner must have a valid driver's license at the time the car is awarded. Trips are subject to space and departure availability. Certain black-out dates may apply. Travel must be completed within one year from the time the prize is awarded. Minors must be accompanied by an adult. Prizes won by minors will be awarded in the name of parent or legal guardian.

For a list of Major Prize Winners (available after 7/30/93): send a self-addressed, stamped envelope entirely separate from your entry to: Winners Classic Sweepstakes Winners, P.O. Box 825, Gibbstown, NJ 08027. Requests must be received by 6/1/93. DO NOT SEND ANY OTHER CORRESPONDENCE TO THIS P.O. BOX.